He'd Made Her An Offer
She'd Be Crazy To Refuse.

"Emily, say you'll be a nanny to Joshua. The hours are flexible. You can double your previous pay." Mitch paused. "Joshua misses you."

Those three words widened the crack in Emily's defenses.

"There's no need to live in," he said evenly. "If that's what's bothering you."

Her heart lurched. Of course he wouldn't want her in his house, not when she might do something inappropriate and embarrassing such as, say, climb into his bed. Again.

She had no choice but to refuse. "No, Mitch, I don't want the job."

He stared at her for what seemed like hours before speaking. "I won't give up, Emily. Take a few days to think about it, to decide what it would take to engage your services. You know you can name your price."

She didn't need a few days to think, didn't even need a few seconds. The answer vibrated through her body and centered in her heart, as sure and strong and passionate as always.

Your love, Mitch Goodwin. That's all it would take.

Dear Reader,

Thanks so much for choosing Silhouette Desire—*the*
destination for powerful, passionate and provocative
love stories. Things start heating up this month with
Katherine Garbera's *Sin City Wedding*, the next installment
of our DYNASTIES: THE DANFORTHS series. An affair,
a secret child, a quickie Las Vegas wedding…and that's just
the beginning of this romantic tale.

Also this month we have the marvelous Dixie Browning with
her steamy *Driven to Distraction*. Cathleen Galitz brings us
another book in the TEXAS CATTLEMAN'S CLUB: THE
STOLEN BABY series with *Pretending with the Playboy*.
Susan Crosby's BEHIND CLOSED DOORS miniseries
continues with the superhot *Private Indiscretions*. And
Bronwyn Jameson takes us to Australia in *A Tempting
Engagement*.

Finally, welcome the fabulous Roxanne St. Claire to
the Silhouette Desire family. We're positive you'll enjoy
Like a Hurricane and will be wanting the other McGrath
brothers' stories. We'll be bringing them to you in the months
to come as well as stories from Beverly Barton, Ann Major
and *New York Times* bestselling author Lisa Jackson. So
keep coming back for more from Silhouette Desire.

More passion to you!

Melissa Jeglinski

Melissa Jeglinski
Senior Editor
Silhouette Desire

Please address questions and book requests to:
Silhouette Reader Service
U.S.: 3010 Walden Ave., P.O. Box 1325, Buffalo, NY 14269
Canadian: P.O. Box 609, Fort Erie, Ont. L2A 5X3

A Tempting Engagement

BRONWYN JAMESON

Silhouette® Desire

Published by Silhouette Books

America's Publisher of Contemporary Romance

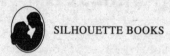 SILHOUETTE BOOKS

ISBN 0-373-76571-1

A TEMPTING ENGAGEMENT

Copyright © 2004 by Bronwyn Turner

Printed in U.S.A.

Books by Bronwyn Jameson

Silhouette Desire

In Bed with the Boss's Daughter #1380
Addicted to Nick #1410
Zane: The Wild One #1452
Quade: The Irresistible One #1487
A Tempting Engagement #1571

BRONWYN JAMESON

spent much of her childhood with her head buried in a book. As a teenager, she discovered romance novels, and it was only a matter of time before she turned her love of reading them into a love of writing them. Bronwyn shares an idyllic piece of the Australian farming heartland with her husband and three sons, a thousand sheep, a dozen horses, assorted wildlife and one kelpie dog. She still chooses to spend her limited downtime with a good book. Bronwyn loves to hear from readers. Write to her at bronwyn@bronwynjameson.com.

For my good mates Lisa, Kim and Yvonne—
thanks for the brainstorming and for your friendship.

One

Emily—his Emily—was working in a bar?

Everything inside Mitch Goodwin tensed at his sister's casually delivered piece of news. Chantal was kidding, right? Looking to get a rise out of big brother on his first night back in Plenty. Welcome home to Australia, Mitch. Now you've unpacked and enjoyed a nice neighborly dinner, here's something to get your blood pumping.

And of all things guaranteed to get his blood pumping, his son's former nanny topped the list. With careful control he slotted another plate into the dishwasher. "And you didn't think you should mention this development when you rang me? When you said 'Guess who's moved back to Plenty?' and I asked how she was doing?"

"*How,* not *what,*" Chantal corrected mildly.

"You said she was fine."

"A change of occupation doesn't necessarily mean a person's not fine and/or dandy."

Mitch gave up all pretence of calm and slammed the dishwasher door shut. "The back bar of the Lion is some kind of change."

"Hey, it's not so bad since Bob Foley took over. As a matter of fact, the last brawl—"

"I don't give a damn if it's the Ritz. She's a trained nanny, for cripe's sake, not a barmaid!"

His angry outburst stopped Chantal midstride. For several surprised seconds she stared at him, the coffee cups in her hands suspended midway between cupboard and bench. "I thought that information would interest you in a more positive way. As in, you moved back here to write, you need a good nanny."

Precisely. And knowing that the best nanny was pulling beers in the town's seediest pub added urgency to his objective as well as heat to his conscience. "Joshua can stay here with you and Quade for an hour or two?" he asked.

"Of course," Chantal answered automatically before she saw him start for the door. Then she threw down a handful of teaspoons with a metallic clatter. "Wait there, just one minute."

Hand on the doorknob, he started counting down the sixty seconds.

"You've been driving half the day, cleaning and unpacking for the rest of it. Go home and sleep. Introduce yourself to a razor and see Emily tomorrow when you're not looking quite so primitive." She paused, eyes narrowing as she studied him head to foot. "I assume you do want to engage her services?"

No, *want* didn't really cover it. He *needed* Emily. He and Joshua both.

That steely determination must have shown in his expression because Chantal sighed and shook her head. ''Go easy on her, Mitch. I know you've had a tough couple of years, but so has Emily.''

Mitch knew all about Emily Warner's tough years, and the fifteen-minute drive into Plenty provided plenty of time for that knowledge to turn him inside out. His ex-wife dismissing her as Joshua's nanny for no good reason. Her grandfather's death and the subsequent battle over his estate. That injustice still boiled Mitch's blood…although not half as much as his own error of judgment.

Error of judgment? He snorted with self-disgust. That didn't even begin to describe how he'd abused his duty of care two months after reemploying her, how he'd taken advantage of her warm, compassionate nature and shattered her trust.

As Joshua's nanny, she'd lived in his home, and the night he learned of Annabelle's death… His hands tightened on the wheel reflexively. He remembered the gut-kick of intense, impotent anger and the numbness he sought at his local bar. Emily had fetched him home, Emily with her gentle brown eyes and her comforting arms and her soft words of sympathy.

He'd kissed her, possibly to shut off those platitudes. Possibly because he'd ached to lose himself in something softer and sweeter and more supportive than a whiskey bottle. Oh, yeah, he remembered the kissing and the falling into bed and then…a dark, black hole in his memory.

A vision of Emily as he'd last seen her, dressed in nothing but his white linen sheets and a soft, pink flush, drifted through his thoughts and rubbed every

raw edge of his conscience. He might not recall what
happened that night, but he would never forget the
morning after. Her wariness, his clumsy questioning,
her insistence that nothing had happened. Except, hot
on the heels of that "nothing"—while he and Joshua
were traveling to Annabelle's funeral—she packed
her bags and disappeared.

Frustration twisted his gut into a tight, hot knot as
he pulled into the car park behind the Lion and
switched off the engine. Six months wondering and
worrying over the consequences of that night, and he
didn't think he could wait another minute, certainly
not the hour until closing. From the near-empty lot
he figured she wouldn't be too busy—the impending
rain had kept most sane folk home. He jumped down
from the cab, shut the door and—city habit—paused
to lock up. He almost missed the small, female figure
that slipped from a side entrance. As she hurried off
down the street, the wind tore at her hooded parka.
Long hair, stick straight, shone silvery pale under a
streetlight.

Emily.

His pulse kicked, an instant response to the tumult
of sensations that swamped his body. Most of them
he didn't want to identify, so he concentrated on the
quick surge of anger. She was walking home alone,
through the dark streets, and she didn't even have the
sense to pull her hood over that luminous beacon of
hair. Might as well shout, Here I am, young, blond
and female. Come and get me.

Suddenly the door to the bar swung open, and two
men veered toward Mitch, two men he recognized as
former classmates at Plenty High. He had nowhere to
hide as Dean Mancini did a classic double take.

"Mitch Goodwin? Stone the crows! I heard you were coming back. Moving into the old Heaslip place, aren't you?"

"That's right." Beyond the mens' shoulders, Mitch could see Emily's rapidly retreating figure. "Sorry, mate, but I—"

"Lucky break, your sister getting married and letting you take her place." Rocky O'Shea rode right over the top of Mitch's attempt to end the conversation. "But then you always were a lucky bastard."

Dean planted an elbow in his mate's side and Rocky, eventually, caught on. His gaze skittered, his Adam's apple bobbed, and Mitch didn't really want to hear whatever fumbling words came next. "I have to be somewhere," he said shortly. "Catch you another time."

Dean cleared his throat. "Sorry about your…you know."

"My ex-wife?"

Both men shifted their feet, awkward and ill at ease, but Mitch was already climbing into his truck. Powerful engine gunning, he wheeled the vehicle into the street, but his irritation faded as quickly as it had flared, replaced by a tinge of sympathy for the discomfited pair.

What were you supposed to say to a man whose wife ran off to chase her dazzling career without a thought for their three-year-old son? A wife whose glamorous must-have lifestyle placed her in a doomed jet in a Caribbean thunderstorm?

Even six months after her funeral, he didn't know what the hell kind of etiquette covered that.

When the first spots of rain dotted the pavement a block from home, Emily huddled deeper into her parka and walked more briskly. She didn't run. Running would be like ceding defeat to the fear crouched low in her belly, woken by the dreaded combination of rain and darkness and the revving of a powerful motor.

"For pity's sake, Emily Jane, you're not even *in* the car," she muttered. "Plus you're in Plenty, not Sydney." Reasonable points, but the sweep of headlights turning into her street sent her memory into a tailspin.

Her car stopped at traffic lights. The door wrenched open. The man, the knife, the icy clutch of terror as he told her to drive.

Emily was jolted back to the present by the sound of a vehicle slowing and pulling into the curb behind her. *Now* she should run but her stupid, scared legs refused to cooperate.

"Emily."

At the sound of her name—of *that* voice—her heart stuttered, then resumed at the same frantic pace, except with a different kind of panic. A Mitch Goodwin kind of panic. She'd heard talk of his imminent move from Sydney to his family's hometown, had known he wouldn't let sleeping dogs—or nannies—lie. That was Mitch's way, ever the journalist, needing the full story, fact by painful fact.

Six months she had spent constructing her version, preparing for this moment, and now her brain appeared to be in meltdown. Wonderful. With a fatalistic sense of doom, she turned toward the car…correction, *truck*. Mitch Goodwin sat behind the wheel of a crew-cab truck that could have been tailor-made. Big, dark, rugged. A shivery tension weakened her limbs as he stretched across the front seat to open the passenger door. The cabin light cast tricky shadows across his darkly stubbled face, and his deep-set eyes, too, looked unfathomably dark. Emily tried not to stare at his lips, not to remember their determined heat as they—

"Get in," those lips said. "It's starting to rain."

Her first reaction, innate, unthinking, was to get in. Emily Warner, always eager to please, to avoid conflict and make life easy for herself and those around her. But the combination of his arrogant demand— "Would you like a ride?" or even "Get in, please," may have worked—and a festering pique set her back on her heels. She was angry about him appearing without forewarning, for following and scaring the daylights out of her, and she was more furious with herself for reacting as always—same old want, same old need.

"You're getting wet." Curt, impatient.

"I did notice that, actually." She lifted her face, and a score of heavy raindrops spattered her heated skin. "But I don't have far to go and I would rather walk."

She didn't run, she walked, and when his truck door slammed, she barely flinched. When he grabbed her arm and swung her around to face him, she did flinch. His gaze narrowed but he didn't let her go, and she was mad enough to lift her chin and glare right back at him. "What do you want, Mitch?"

"To get you out of this rain," Mitch fired back, burning from the way she'd refused his lift and jumped from his touch.

"Then perhaps you had best let go of my arm."

He lost all patience. Tightening his hold, he ushered her the last thirty yards, through her front gate and onto the sheltering verandah. When he tipped her face to catch the glow of a nearby streetlight, a raw tightness gripped his gut. Her skin felt as baby soft as he remembered, but her face looked strained with a new weariness. And her eyes...still deep, warm, mellow, but no longer trusting. They shifted under his scrutiny, her expression edged with a wariness he'd seen only once before.

That morning in his bed. Damn.

"You've been working too hard," he muttered, stroking the dark circle under one eye with the pad of his thumb. Wishing he could erase it along with that leap of reaction in her wide eyes. Fear?

When he let her go, she backed up so quickly she almost tripped over her feet. Mitch's gut twisted with consternation. "What's the matter, Emily? Why are you so jumpy?"

That chased the wariness from her eyes. "You drove up behind me and scared me half to death. You manhandled me into my own yard. Do you really have to ask?"

Put like that... "I'm sorry for frightening you. I meant to catch you before you left the pub."

Distrust darkened her gaze but she didn't look away. "Why? What do you want, Mitch?"

The directness of her question swept all contrition aside, leaving only the hot, churning frustration born of seeing her again. "Why did you run away, Emily?"

"I left a note—"

"That said absolutely nothing except sorry. What was that supposed to mean? Sorry, Joshua, for leaving and breaking your heart?"

She flinched as if he'd grabbed her again, as if he'd struck her, and stared at him with wide, stunned eyes. Hell. He hadn't meant such a low blow. Undeserved, given her reason for running. He raked a hand through his hair, scraping the wet strands back from his face and wishing he could tidy up his rampant emotions as easily.

"I'm sorry, Em." He closed his eyes a moment. "That was uncalled for."

When she didn't answer, he looked back to find she'd sat. On top of a packing box. Distracted, he gestured at its many mates sitting higgledy-piggledy along the porch. "Are you moving?"

"Yes." Her reply sounded as much like a weary sigh as a word.

Mitch frowned. Chantal hadn't mentioned this in her update. "Because of your grandfather's will?"

"*Step*grandfather."

"Semantics. Every man and his dog knows you did more for Owen in his last years than all his blood relatives lumped together. You shouldn't have given up fighting, Emily."

"I didn't give up, I lost," she fired back. Defiance lent color to her cheeks; her eyes sparked fiercely. She no longer looked stunned, no longer sounded defeated. If he touched her now, she wouldn't jump and tremble. If he touched her now... *Don't go there, Mitch.*

He blew out a long, serrated breath and hitched his chin toward the boxes. "When are you moving?"

"This weekend."

"To?"

"I have a room at the Lion." She stood up and straightened defensively, as if in response to something she saw in his eyes. Possibly pure, hot exasperation. "It's clean and it's conveni—"

"It's cold, and there's nothing convenient about living on top of a bar. Hell, Emily. You about jumped out of your skin when I drove up beside you. How do you think you're going to manage when a drunk knocks on your door?"

"I've taken self-defence classes," she said, lifting her chin. But the words came out coated in hesitation rather than bravado. With a jolt of satisfaction Mitch sensed the shift, and started toward her. No way was she moving into any hotel room, and he intended to make that crystal clear.

"What did they teach you, Emily?" he asked softly, backing her up with slow, steady deliberation. "Did they teach you the three prime targets?"

"Yesss."

Her husky whisper wouldn't have scared a mouse. Disgusted, annoyed, he kept coming. "Which would you go for first?"

Her back hit the wall and her eyes widened, thick lashes fluttering. Her mouth opened, no words came out, but Mitch felt the touch of her exhalation against his skin. And knew he was much closer than he'd intended.

She shifted, drawing breath, and her jacket brushed against his, a soft shush of fabric against fabric, yet he felt it as intensely as if he'd leaned right into her body. An intense desire to do just that expanded in his blood, catching him completely unaware. Hands planted either side of her face, he felt the soft temptation of her body inches from his. Saw her lips, pink, moist, open.

You're supposed to be talking her into coming back, he told himself, not reminding her why she left.

"What would you do, Emily?" he asked, irritated with himself, his body, his cursed male hormones. "If I were that intruder?"

Blinking, she stretched taller against the wall, and he wondered if she was trying to escape or trying to get closer. Mouth to mouth. And still she said nothing, did nothing but breathe fast and shallow, air sloughing against his throat until he could stand it no longer. With a muttered oath, he used his purchase on the wall to push himself away.

From the edge of the porch, he heard her sigh, the sound as soft as the slow fall of rain. "I guess you made your point."

"Which point would that be?" he asked with rueful honesty. Something like—now I've seen you in my bed, I can't think of anything else but getting you back there?

"The lessons were a big fat waste of money. I am a wimp and nothing will change that." She tried to temper the words with a smile, but when Mitch didn't return it, she looked away. "The room is only temporary. Until I find a better place."

"You don't have to do that," he said slowly. This was it—the opening he'd been waiting for. He paused, deliberately, until her gaze swung back to his. "If you come back and work for me."

At first she simply shook her head, eyes hauntingly dark with some unnamed emotion. But when he opened his mouth to explain, she stepped in quickly. "I have a job. Two jobs, actually."

"Chantal told me about the bar job." Mitch shook

his head, hoping to clear it of the residual, hazy desire. "What else are you doing?"

"Cleaning. At the Lion."

"Pulling beer and cleaning hotel rooms?" The words exploded from his mouth. "Hell, Emily, that's not the kind of work you should be doing."

Hell, Mitch, that's not the way to go about this. What is wrong with you? Scaring her out of her wits, all but jumping her bones, judging her job choice…or lack of choice. He needed to remember what this was about. Joshua needed a secure and stable home environment, constancy and routine, and he wanted Emily. Mitch had let him down enough times this past year—this time, he wouldn't fail.

"Joshua needs a nanny," he said more softly. Evenly. "I'm working from home, writing, so the hours are flexible. My *Everyday Heroes* series is going into production soon, so I'll have trips to Sydney where I might be away most of the week. I'll make the extra hours worth your while. You can double your previous pay."

She choked out a laugh, a strangled sound of surprise. "With that kind of pay, you should have candidates lined up halfway to Cliffton."

"I'm only making the offer to you."

Her amusement faded, her eyes looked large and somber in the low light, and when she spoke, the one word was barely audible. "Why?"

"Joshua wants you."

Those three words widened the crack in Emily's defences—the crack that had started when he'd accused her of breaking Joshua's heart. Not knowing how to answer—not wanting to answer too fast, too emotionally, too thoughtlessly—she touched an anxious hand to her throat.

"Ever since you left, he's been…difficult."

Oh, Lord, he knew exactly where it hurt most. Emily's gaze darted back to his shadowed face, found his expression as hard to read as the color of his eyes. Hazel, according to his passport, but they changed as often as his mood. One minute as green as a winter garden, the next the cool gray of a rainstorm.

"There's no need to live in," he said evenly. "If that's what's bothering you."

Her heart lurched. Of course he wouldn't want her in his house, not when she might do something inappropriate and embarrassing such as, say, climb into his bed. Again.

"I'll find you a place in town and pay the rent."

"As well as that extra pay?" She swallowed audibly. "You are kidding, right?"

"Do I look like I am?"

No, he looked intent and purposeful, his jaw set as hard as the rest of his body. A ripple of sensation shimmered through her nerve endings as she recalled the look in his eyes as he'd tracked her across the porch. The feeling of all that dark heat so close, and so far. Because naturally, she'd misread those signals, too. He'd been playing with her, proving his point, demonstrating her vulnerability.

Frustrated and annoyed, she shook her head. "That's plain ridiculous, spending so much money—"

"Money isn't the issue. I'll pay whatever it takes, Emily."

A strangled, hiccuping laugh escaped her lips at the irony. He'd pay whatever it took, and no amount of money could compensate her deficit. His house was twelve miles from town, and she couldn't bring herself to sit behind the steering wheel, not once since the carjacking. "I can't drive, Mitch. I don't have a car."

"What happened to your Kia?"

"I needed the money for my legal bills," she said simply. The insurance money for her burned-out car, dumped at the end of a terrifying joy ride. But that wasn't something she had shared—or would share—with anyone. "And before you offer to buy me a new car, I should add that it won't make a lick of difference. The answer is no."

A word he apparently didn't understand because, after the barest beat of a pause, he kept right on. "You can stay with Quade and Chantal. It's not a long walk across the paddocks and they have—"

Anger flashed, quick and hot. "No, Mitch."

He stilled, straightened, tensed. *She* had surprised *him,* she noted with a spurt of pride. Dark frustration burned in his eyes right alongside fierce determination. "Fine. We'll find somewhere else."

"I meant, no, I don't want the job."

For an instant he looked too taken aback to respond, then he drew a hand down his face, the gesture so achingly familiar she felt its kick in the solar plexus. "What can I offer to change your mind?" he asked softly.

Emily shook her head. "I'm sorry, Mitch."

Breath held, she waited for him to say more. She could see the more in his expression, in the firm set of his jaw. She knew how stubborn he could be.

"I'm not giving up, Emily. Take a few days to

think about it, to decide what it would take to engage your services. You know you can name your price.''

As she watched him walk away, she shook her head sadly. She didn't need a few days to think, didn't even need a few seconds. The answer vibrated through her body and centered in her heart, as sure and strong and passionate as always.

Your love, Mitch Goodwin. That's all it would take.

Two

"Emmy, Emmy, Emmy."

Emily had scarcely opened the door before a pair of surprisingly strong four-year-old arms wrapped themselves around her legs. Their owner didn't stop talking, thirteen to the dozen, his run-on words indistinguishable, given the way he'd buried his face and a large part of his body in her cumbersome winter bathrobe.

Oh, and *perhaps* her hearing was hampered slightly by the treacherous buzzing in her ears, a reaction to both the warm enthusiasm of Joshua's welcome and locking gazes with the second of her early-morning visitors.

Six foot two of clean-shaven, square-jawed purpose.

Beneath her thick, flannel robe and not-so-thick satin pajamas, Emily's tummy flipped. "Oh," she said. Then, even more intelligently, "I wasn't expecting you."

"Were you expecting someone else?" Hazel eyes slid over her, devastatingly direct.

"No one." Absolutely no one.

"We're here to help," Joshua said. "In our truck."

Emily fastened both hands around her coffee mug, anchoring herself against this latest thunderbolt. They were here—unannounced, no forewarning—to help her move. Mitch and his backup weapon, a three-foot-tall pistol of a kid who still hadn't disengaged himself from her clothes. She ached to sink down and hug him back, but feared she wouldn't be able to let go.

Or that she might totally let go, releasing all the pent-up emotions swirling inside and catching at her throat and the back of her eyes. Three days ago this man had flabbergasted her with his crazy, name-your-price job offer yet it seemed more like three weeks. So much had happened since, events that had brought her life to a crippling new low.

Mitch Goodwin sure could pick his times.

"You should have rung first," she said. "I could have saved you the trip into town."

The words came out more tersely than she'd intended, and Mitch's gaze narrowed in response, although his expression lost none of its determination. A shiver rocketed up her spine. Standing on her porch in the pearl-edged winter sunlight, he should not have looked so steely hard. Hard eyes, hard face, hard body.

"You're not finished packing?" he asked, hard voiced.

"I'm not moving." Emily allowed herself one

small luxury, one hand on Joshua's head, one fleeting caress of his silky hair. "Not today, at least."

"Because you lost your job?"

Emily's hand stilled, although she had no reason for surprise. In a town such as Plenty news traveled fast, bad news even faster, and with all the cosmic forces currently conspiring against her, it made sense for Mitch to turn up on her doorstep…while she was at her most vulnerable.

"I didn't only lose the job," she said. There seemed little point in hiding the truth. "I also lost the room."

"Emmy, did you really sock that moron?" Joshua asked.

While the father admonished the son for his language, she closed her eyes. Shook her head. "I didn't sock anyone, sweetie."

"But Uncle Zane said—"

"Too much," Mitch finished. "He also said he's seen you out walking a dog."

"Was he right, Emmy? Have you got a dog?" Instantly diverted, Joshua fizzed with excitement. "Is he black and white like Mac? Didya know Uncle Zane's keeping Mac 'cuz he's grown 'tached? That's what Daddy said. Is he a she? Is he big?"

Emily squatted down to four-year-old level and waited for him to draw breath. "He's a bitzer, not as big as your Mac, but just as smart. His name is Digger."

"Where is he?"

"In the yard out back."

"Can I see him?" His eyes, so like his father's, pleaded with hers. Oh, boy, she was in some trouble if he started asking for things other than viewing her gramps's dog. "Please, Emmy?"

"Let's see what your dad says." She looked up past long denim-encased legs, hands in pockets— *Don't look there, Emily Jane!*—and a sky-blue sweater she'd always fancied. Perhaps because of the way it stretched across his broad, beautiful chest. She swallowed to find her voice. "He's used to kids. The Connorses next door took him after Gramps died, until they moved."

"Okay, but make sure you…" Mitch's voice petered out as Joshua sprinted across the porch and disappeared around the corner. "Is there a fence to negotiate?"

"There's a gate. He'll manage."

Excited barking announced his success, and Emily was suddenly very conscious of being alone with Mitch. Despite the broad daylight, she felt more self-aware than the other night in the rain and dark. With every movement she felt the gentle slide of satin nightwear against her skin. Hoped he couldn't see the effect of that stimulation through her thick robe. She folded her arms across her chest and tried to remember what they'd been talking about before the dog distraction.

"So, you didn't sock the moron?"

Now she remembered. Unfortunately. A flush warmed her cheeks from the inside out. "I didn't touch him, I only threatened to—"

"Did he touch you?"

Emily shook her head. "I don't know what you heard, but I'm sure at least fifty percent is exaggerated."

"Suppose you tell me which bits are true?"

Ahh, that protectiveness. She heard it in his grim voice, saw it in the tight set of his jaw and wished she didn't find it quite so bone-meltingly appealing. She wanted to be strong, wanted to stand up for herself and develop some backbone, but every time she was put to the test lately, she managed to fail.

"This traveler was trying to chat me up in the bar. Harmless stuff," she said quickly when his eyes darkened. "I didn't think anything of it, but then he was waiting when I finished my shift and, well, I told him I wasn't interested."

"Did he touch you?" he asked again.

"No." She shook her head, surprised by his vehemence. "It was nothing, Mitch, really."

"If it was nothing, how did you come to lose your job?"

"Maybe I walked under a ladder or a black cat." Emily faked a laugh. "It's like bad luck's following me around."

"What happened, Emily?"

Mitch Goodwin in journalist mode made a formidable opponent. He kept on ferreting around, circling and digging. She might as well get it over with, the whole belittling truth. "The next day he told my boss that some money was taken from his room. I cleaned it, so I was the scapegoat."

Mitch swore. "You were sacked on this jerk's say-so? Because you rejected him?"

It sounded bad, put like that, but at the time she'd almost understood her boss's dilemma. She hated it, but she'd understood. "His company does a lot of business with the hotel. I guess they didn't want to lose it."

"So you're just going to take this?" Their eyes met and held, his as dark and angry as a winter storm.

"I know I should do something, and if it didn't involve conflict, I would. But these last months with Gramps's will and his family and all…"

"Chantal told me about that. I'm sorry, Em."

She sighed and shook her head. "I'm just tired of fighting."

Something shifted in his eyes and he nodded, as if with satisfaction. "I'm pleased to hear that."

Then, before she realized what he was about, he strode along her porch, hunkered down in a way that threatened the seams of his jeans and lifted the first of her packed boxes.

When he started back the way he'd come, Emily jumped into his path. "What are you doing?"

His look was an undisguised challenge. "Are we fighting about this or not?"

"Yes." She tugged at the box, but he held firm. "No." She released her grip and a heavy sigh. "I don't know."

There was something incredibly undignified, not to mention futile, about playing tug-of-war with a man nine inches taller and at least forty pounds heavier. Especially while dressed in one's nightwear. Emily lifted a hand to tuck a loose tress of hair behind her ear and felt him looking. Not at her hair. Face flushing, she pulled the gaping sides of her robe back together and tightened the sash at her waist.

He used her momentary distraction to haul the box off to his truck. When he came back for a second load, she stepped in front of him. "Where do you think you're taking my things?"

"Chantal's."

"Wait."

Naturally, being Mitch Goodwin on a mission, he paid no notice. Not until she stopped him with a hand on his arm. For a moment she lost her place. Her senses focused on the rigid strength of his muscles, taut under the heavy load, and her memories of touching him another time. Without the barrier of a soft woolen sweater.

He cleared his throat and she snatched her hand away.

"You can't just move me somewhere," she said, her voice husky with rising heat and panic. This was so much worse than she'd imagined, being close to him, touching, remembering. "Does your sister know?"

"She made the offer."

Because Mitch asked? Maybe. The Goodwins—unlike *her* splintered family—supported each other unfailingly. Or perhaps Chantal, who'd been her lawyer at the start of the estate wrangle, did offer without any prompting. Even after off-loading Emily's case to a city estate specialist, her support and help continued. But she and Cameron Quade were newlyweds with a baby on the way. They deserved their own space. She shook her head. "I don't want to move in with them."

"Where do you want to move then? It has to be somewhere…unless you want me to buy this place for you."

Heart pounding, she read the direct challenge in his eyes. This is why he'd come, to offer this choice— his sister's charity or his.

Standing so close, with the feel of his hard strength still coursing through her veins, with the scent of some masculine soap in her nostrils, she knew she had no choice. At least Chantal might provide some respite, some thinking time.

Gazes still locked, she drew a short, sharp breath and stepped aside. She didn't need to say a word. A small nod signaled his satisfaction, and he got on with the job, one box after another. Feeling utterly defeated, Emily started to sink down on the top step, then thought better of it. He might just pick her up like one of the boxes and dump her in the truck.

She needed to get dressed, preferably in the kind of thick, winter clothing that might numb his potent effect, or at least keep her responses contained. Then she needed to check on Joshua and Digger before they found mischief.

Five minutes later she watched them scamper around Gramps's big yard, a hairy tricolored mutt and a boy whose laughter soared, as pure as the winter sunshine. A surge of tenderness rushed through her, so huge it rendered her dizzy. She rested her chin atop her arms on the chest-high fence and let her heart enjoy the moment.

How could he have known? How could he have picked this perfect time and this perfect blond-haired accomplice?

Oh, it wasn't only Joshua who got to her, but the whole father-son package. It would be so easy to capitulate, to talk herself into the benefits of a secure job with a mind-boggling pay packet. To succumb to the seductive knowledge that they needed her in all the everyday practical ways, that they wanted *her*— plain, old, vanilla variety Emily Jane Warner—ahead of anyone else.

Except that after she tumbled completely and impractically under their spell came the heartbreaking truth that she was only the nanny and could never replace the beautiful, exotic, triple-choc-and-mocha Annabelle. All she needed to do was remember the pain of his point-blank rejection. In his bed, naked and willing, and he'd turned away. She wouldn't set herself up for another bout of humiliation and heartache, not of that magnitude, not ever again.

A low ache settled in the pit of her stomach when she sensed Mitch's approach, his footsteps muted by the thick, damp lawn. He rested his hands on top of the fence next to hers, and side by side they watched Joshua climb into an old tire slung from a tree in the far corner of the yard. Digger yapped gleefully as he tracked the swing's motion, back and forth, back and forth.

"It's *zactly* like Uncle Zane's swing," Joshua yelled, clearly delighted with the discovery.

She sneaked in a sideways glance and caught the ghost of a smile on Mitch's lips. Pleasure, pure and strong, pierced her chest. She remembered his companionship with his own dog, back in the days before Annabelle decided they needed an upmarket apartment and that she might be allergic to dogs.

"I'm surprised you let Zane keep Mac."

His shrug brushed against her shoulder. "Well, he'd grown 'tached."

She smiled at the echo of Joshua's words and didn't need another glance to know he shared the smile. Ahh, she missed these moments. There'd been so many in those first years, so much warmth and understanding.

"He ran away."

For a moment she thought she'd misheard his low words. "*Joshua* ran away?"

"At the mall." Mitch expelled a harsh breath. "He was there with the nanny."

"When?" Alarm tightened her throat, so the question came out as a husky squeak.

"Two weeks ago. It took three hours to find him."

Emily struggled to accept what he was telling her. "That doesn't sound like Joshua. Why would he do that?"

Mitch didn't answer for so long that she thought he wouldn't…or couldn't. Then his sleeve brushed against hers again, although this time it wasn't a casual shrug but a tightening of muscles. Everything inside her tensed in reaction. "He thought he saw you. The nanny called after him but he kept on running and she lost him in the crowd."

Not your fault, Emily Jane, not your problem, she told herself, but guilt swamped logic. Fingers pressed against her lips, she whispered, "I'm sorry."

Sorry for Mitch's despair, sorry for leaving and breaking Joshua's heart. Sorry even for the hapless nanny.

"And this is why you moved back here?" she asked quietly. "Why you want me to come back and work for you?"

"I'll do anything to stop that happening again. Anything."

The steel-capped purpose in his voice should have alarmed Emily, could have intimidated her. But all she heard was the sentiment behind the words, and when she placed a comforting hand on his forearm, she didn't feel hard muscles and heat. She felt his vulnerability as a father, the fear and helplessness he must have suffered in those three hours.

"It's been a rough time for him," she said quietly. A rough time for both of you. "Does he...talk about his mother?"

In the hard plane of his cheek, a muscle jumped. "Not often. You know she wasn't around much."

Yes, but the impact of her leaving, her death, must have scored painfully deep. Much deeper than her own departure. "She was his mother," Emily said simply. Under her hand his arm twitched with tension and she increased the pressure in a gesture of comfort and support. A pittance, she knew, given the depth of his grief. "No matter where she was."

He opened his mouth to reply, closed it again. Emily's heart stalled, waited, longed for him to share. *Dangerous,* her mind whispered. Remember the last time you offered comfort? *Remember that heartache?*

Lost in the intensity of the moment, she didn't hear Joshua until he was right at the fence, his small hand tugging at her sweater to attract her attention. "You're right, Emmy. Digger *is* a smart dog. Watch this, Daddy."

He tossed a much-chewed tennis ball long and straight, a sportsman in the making, his father's son. They applauded the retrieval part of the act, even though Digger absconded with the ball, circling the yard and refusing to give up his toy.

"See, Daddy? He doesn't give it back when he wants to play chasies."

Eventually Joshua gave up the chase, falling flat on his back at their feet. A small boy filled with exuberance, happy and exhausted from the simplest kind of play, not thinking about the mother who deserted him. Emily's heart twisted with sympathy. Her own mother might still be alive, but she knew all about that kind of rejection.

"After we take your stuff to Chantal's," the boy said, puffing from his supine position, "we're going shopping. Can you come with us? We hate shopping."

"Why is that?"

He rolled his eyes. "Last time, Mrs. Hertzy patted me on the head. I'm not a dog."

"You smell like one."

He laughed uproariously and Emily was doomed. This kid...how could she turn her back on him?

"But we've got to shop," he continued with breathless sincerity. "We're sick of eating s'getti."

At which point Digger dropped the slobbery ball on his new friend's chest, his eyes lambent with come-play pleading. Batteries recharged, Joshua leaped to his feet and took off again. As she watched him run, Emily felt her own peculiar sense of breathlessness. She shook her head.

"What?" Mitch asked, and she turned to catch him watching her, his expression tricky.

"'We hate shopping. We're sick of spaghetti.' Have you been coaching him?" she asked.

A corner of his very attractive mouth kicked up. "He has a point about the head patting."

"They do that to you, too?" she asked, tongue in cheek.

He didn't laugh. "I'd pay you triple just to avoid the supermarket."

Oh, yes, she saw it very clearly now. The pained looks of pity and tuttings of sympathy for "that poor Mitch Goodwin whose wife up and left." How he must hate that. And, oh, how she ached to help. She felt herself wavering, the need churning and building and crying out for her to accept.

"I'm no use to you as a shopper," she said, striving for a light tone. "Unless you think I can wheel one of those trolleys all the way out to your place."

"You know I'll provide a car."

"I don't drive." There, she'd said it. The truth. And she turned her gaze to Joshua climbing into the tree swing again.

"You used to drive just fine," Mitch said slowly. "What happened, did you have an accident and lose your nerve?"

"Something like that."

"Then you just need to retrain."

She blew out a scoffing breath and shook her head. "You just need to force me behind the wheel of a car, first."

"I'll get you driving again, Emily."

That confidence—he was a man who thrived on accomplishment—could have convinced most people. Except Emily knew how easily she froze, not every time but with certain combinations of stimuli. Darkness, city streets, a male passenger, the strident sound of an overrevved engine.

She didn't know what to say or how to explain her problem with driving. Remembering his vehemence when she'd told him about losing her job...no, she could not add this story to her growing inventory of victimhood. He would ask more questions, demand more answers, when all she wanted was to forget the whole episode. When all she wanted—just one blessed time—was to feel strong and in control.

Agreeing to work for Mitch Goodwin did not seem

like a wonderful step in that direction. She exhaled on a ragged sigh just as Joshua scampered back to unwittingly tighten the screws. "Can Digger come and live with us, too?" he asked.

Oh, boy. Emily hunkered down to his level. "I'm not coming to live with you, sweetie."

"Why?"

Why, indeed? "Because I'm moving in at your aunty Chantal's and uncle Cameron's."

Joshua stared at her hard. "D'you mean Uncle Quade?"

Everyone called him by his surname, why not Joshua? "Yes, I mean your uncle Quade. It's not far from your house if you want to come visit."

"Daddy said I'm not to go 'cross the paddocks."

"That's because he's worried that you might get lost."

Expression solemn, he seemed to consider her point. His eyes were deep, gray-green pools of hope. "Not if I had a smart dog like Digger. *He* wouldn't get lost."

Emily struggled to suppress a grin. The dog might be smart, but Joshua Goodwin was a genius at twisting the conversation. He wanted a dog. Perhaps she didn't have to let him down completely.

"I think it's time you guys got going," she suggested, rising to her feet. "I have to finish packing."

"Is there much more?" Mitch asked.

"Not really." She shoved her hands in her jeans pockets, not wanting to think about the implications. Once she finished packing, there'd be nothing left to do but leave. She would be adrift again, homeless. "Just some clothes and personal things."

"I'll call back in a few hours, then?"

She nodded. Watched as Mitch let his son through the gate, then followed them around to the front of the house. Seeing them together, fair and dark, short and tall, but bonded by blood and love, her own feeling of aloneness swelled from the pit of her stomach, tightening her chest and constricting her throat. She had to sit on her porch steps, had to close her eyes and fight the tears and the clamoring need to call out.

She also had to ask Mitch about the dog.

Taking a deep breath, she rose to her feet as he closed the truck door behind Joshua and started around to the driver's side.

"Mitch."

She waited until he came back, out of Joshua's earshot, one brow raised in query.

"It's about Digger. I can't keep him." The reason didn't need stating—a dog couldn't be packed away in a storage box. "I was thinking that a dog might be good for Joshua."

"It would," he said slowly, but his expression remained closed. Not the good-idea-Emily smile she'd hoped for. His eyes met hers, hard and direct. "But right now he needs something more than a dog. He needs you, Emily. We both do."

Three

Living with Chantal and Cameron Quade wasn't as bad as Emily had imagined. Allowed to housekeep and cook, she didn't feel like a complete charity case, although she had spent the last forty-eight hours on tenterhooks, waiting for her nearest neighbor to resume his recruitment campaign.

He'd been surprisingly silent during the fraught trip from Gramps's to her new temporary residence, although Joshua compensated with his mile-a-minute chatter. She hadn't helped them shop and she hadn't seen either since, yet she remained hyperaware of their presence, a mere mile away, closer, across the three paddocks that separated the farmhouses.

Was it any wonder she jumped every time someone walked into the room?

This time it was Chantal. Yawning widely as she came through the kitchen doorway, she seemed sleepy enough from her afternoon nap not to notice Emily jump. Unfortunately, Chantal had been a lawyer all her adult life and a Goodwin even longer. Even half-awake, she noticed.

"You have to stop doing that while you have a knife in your hand. You'll have a finger off."

Emily studied the paring knife in her hand. No blood. And her fingers were all intact. "I'm sorry. I was thinking of something else and you startled me," she said unnecessarily.

"Well, I kind of hoped I didn't look *that* frightening." With one hand resting comfortably on her pregnant belly, Chantal hitched herself up onto a kitchen stool. "Not with another two months to grow even fatter."

"You know you look beautiful."

"You know you have a friend for life," Chantal countered. Then her expression turned ominously serious. "Is that incident with the jerk at the hotel making you jumpy?"

"No," Emily replied truthfully. Probably too truthfully, seeing as Chantal would now go digging for another explanation. She was very much like her brother in that way.

"What are you making?"

"This soup." Emily pointed to the recipe card on the bench. "Is that all right?"

Chantal laughed. "Anything I don't have to prepare is fine by me."

Emily continued chopping vegetables. What-are-you-making-for-dinner had been a diversion, to settle her down. Questioning would resume shortly.

"I was talking to my brother earlier," the inquisitor

continued with a deceptive casualness that didn't deceive Emily.

Her knife skidded off the side of a carrot. She didn't dare look up, to see the smug satisfaction on Chantal's face at finding the answer to her why-is-Emily-jumpy riddle so easily. Her brother, as always.

"He's concerned about Joshua."

Emily's gaze flew up. "What's wrong? He seemed fine on Sunday."

"He is...and he isn't."

Keep dicing and slicing, Emily. Don't prompt... "Because I won't take my job back?" she blurted, unable to help herself.

Chantal's pause was measured. "Have you almost finished there?"

"For now."

"Great. Get yourself a drink and we'll sit somewhere comfortable. This stool is not big enough for the pregnant version of my butt."

With shaky hands Emily poured two glasses of apple cider and followed Chantal—with crackers and Brie—into the lounge. Easier to hide behind a glass than a knife, she reasoned, should her hostess's cross-examination prove too savvy.

"Let's start at the beginning," Chantal mumbled around her first bite of cheese. "Which, I guess, is back when Annabelle fired you."

"She didn't fire—"

"She didn't find fault with everything you did? She didn't suggest you'd be happier somewhere else?" Chantal waved a dismissive hand at Emily's how-the-heck-did-you-know? look. "Not so clever of me. She was impossible to please."

Emily's heart thudded hard as she wondered where

Chantal was going with the history lesson, but she couldn't not listen. Like a moth to the flame.

"Anyway, Mitch took an in-studio job so he could be home more regular hours, and Joshua went to day care, and they didn't need a live-in nanny."

"Until Annabelle left."

"And while Mitch chased around the world trying to talk her into coming home, Joshua was shuffled around between grandparents and aunts." Chantal looked up as she reached for another cracker. "You know how that feels, don't you?"

Throat tight with compassion, Emily nodded. Oh, yes, she knew all about shuffling. From mother to stepfather to mother to the next stepfather with only Gramps making her feel as though she had a secure home and a modicum of love.

"Which is when you came back into the picture, Emily."

Oh yes, this part she knew all about. The day after his other sister, Julia's, wedding to Zane O'Sullivan, Mitch had come to see her. Less than a week after Gramps's funeral, lost and alone and at her most vulnerable, she'd taken her old job back and prayed that her infatuation with her boss would die…or at least not live long enough to humiliate her.

"What happened after I left?" she asked, eager to skip the humiliation part. Hoping Chantal couldn't hear the skittery beat of her heart.

"Oh, we talked him into getting another nanny. She was hopeless. The next one—"

"There were more?"

"Two more." Smiling wryly, Chantal shook her head. "I suppose you've noticed that my brother is somewhat attractive?"

Somewhat? Emily made a noncommittal sound, sort of a cross between an uh-huh and clearing her throat. Now seemed like the perfect time to hide behind her glass.

"Nanny number two..." Gaze narrowed in concentration, Chantal tapped a nail on her chin. "Her name was Monique, from memory, and she misinterpreted the live-in part of the clause."

While Emily choked on her juice, Chantal laughed with genuine amusement. She reached across and touched Emily's arm, compatriots in gossip.

"Can you imagine Mitch when he found her in his bed?"

"Um...not really."

Liar. She didn't have to imagine, she *knew*. He'd look stunned, then so uncomfortable he couldn't meet her eyes. There'd be a softly muttered expletive, some stony-faced silence, and, finally, with her nerves stretched to snap point, he would start asking questions.

She wondered if Monique had handled them any better than she had done.

"The third nanny is the one Joshua ran away from at the mall?"

Chantal nodded. "After that episode, Mitch accepted my offer to take over the lease on Korringal. We all thought he'd have more luck finding reliable child care here."

Emily rolled her cold glass across one warm cheek and then the other. Finally Chantal was getting to the point. Not a cross-examination, after all, but a sales pitch. She wondered if that's what her brother had been talking to her about earlier, enlisting her help.

"Mitch needs someone he trusts, someone Joshua

loves. I know he can be a giant pain in the neck, but if anyone can put up with him, it's you, Emily.''

For no particular reason—except the sentiment behind those words, the faith, the trust—Emily's eyes misted with tears. She heard Chantal cluck with sympathy, although she watched with her shrewd lawyer's eyes as Emily battled for composure.

''So far—'' she continued quietly ''—we've only talked about what Mitch and Joshua want. What about you, Emily? What do you want?''

What did she want? Apart from the impossible. ''I'm not sure,'' she whispered in true, hesitant, Emily Jane Warner style. Oh, how she hated that tremulous voice and the tears that still prickled the back of her throat. How she wished for the courage to either go after what she wanted, or to tell it—him, them—to go take a flying leap off Mount Tibaroo.

After a long, intense silence Chantal spoke slowly, thoughtfully. ''You know what I think? You've just lost your job and your home, you've been bodily shifted out here and you feel pressured. You're not seeing a lot of choices.''

Oh, yes. That pretty much described her life.

''There's no need to make a decision right off. You can stay here as long as you like—'' She lifted a hand to silence Emily's attempted objection. ''And if you decide you don't want to work for Mitch—and he'll kill me if he finds out I'm saying this!—then that's your choice.''

Choices. What a tempting notion except— ''I can't stay here indefinitely. I need to work, to find another job.''

''I know a lot of people.'' Chantal hitched a shoulder nonchalantly. ''If I ask around, I'm sure I can scare up another nannying job, although it may not be close to Plenty. Does that matter?''

''Only if they need a nanny who drives.'' Her first, tentative flutter of hope took a swan dive. Which parents chose a caregiver who couldn't ferry their kids to school or kindy or the park? Who couldn't, in an emergency, get them to a doctor quickly?

''You didn't sell your car, did you?'' Chantal asked, eyes narrowing with uncanny perception. ''Did you crash it while you were in Sydney? That's it, isn't it? I recognize a fellow victim when I see one.''

''But you're driving again,'' Emily said, remembering Chantal's bad wreck. ''Wasn't that hard, getting back behind the wheel?''

''It took some discipline and practice, but I conquered my fear.'' Chantal reached out again, her touch warm and supportive. ''We'll have you ready for Le Mans before you leave here, Emily.''

''You're seven months pregnant.''

''Quade will do it if I ask nicely.'' Chantal winked. ''If I ask *really* nicely, he might let you drive the sports car.''

The tears returned, this time more a pea-souper fog than a mist. Emily wiped them with the back of her hand, sniffed, smiled shakily. ''Thank you. I don't know why you're doing all this.''

Chantal shrugged. ''Remnant guilt, maybe.''

''*What?*''

''I wanted your case so badly I encouraged you to fight your grandfather's will. I didn't do you any favors, huh?''

''It was my choice, I wanted to do something proactive for a change. You didn't influence my decision.'' Emily paused, remembering Mitch's heated challenge on her porch that first night. "Do you think I gave up too easily? That I should have appealed?"

"That was your choice to make," Chantal said firmly.

"Your brother thinks I did."

"Thinks what?"

At that deep-voiced question they both started and turned. Mitch's height and width filled much of the doorway; his black sweater and dark-stubbled jaw lent him an air of danger, and that awareness swamped Emily in a slow rolling wave.

Mitch noticed that unguarded response, exactly the same as when she had opened her door Sunday morning, pale hair spilling over her shoulders, all pink-faced surprise and soft-eyed temptation. And Mitch reacted in the exact same way now, with sudden, insistent heat.

Damn.

Now wasn't the time to remember that glimpse of pale skin when her robe gaped, the curve of her full breasts or the knowledge that she slept with satin next to her skin. He needed to concentrate on the purpose of his visit. He leaned over the back of the couch and kissed his sister's proffered cheek.

"We were talking about Owen's estate," she explained. "Emily says you think she should have appealed."

"I think she should fight harder for her rights…in some instances." He tilted his head toward the kitchen. "Shouldn't you be making dinner?"

"Nope. Emily's cooking."

He fixed his sister with a meaningful look and her eyes widened in acknowledgment, her lips forming an *okay* as she rose to her feet. "I do have to get you a drink, though."

"Make it a long one."

She winked as she walked by, leaned down to turn on the stereo—so she couldn't inadvertently eavesdrop—and then left them alone. Sometimes his littlest sister was okay. Although…

"Marriage hasn't improved her taste in music," he said as a popular boy-band crooned from the speakers. He crossed the room and turned the volume down a couple of notches before asking, "Have you heard from Bob Foley?"

The hotel owner had been taken aback by Mitch's visit but most helpful. A high-media profile—not to mention a lawyer sister—garnered respect.

Emily looked up, surprised, then not. "I wondered why he rang."

"I assume he rang to apologize."

"I now assume he rang because you told him to." She did not sound happy about his intervention. He didn't care.

"I *suggested* he show a little faith in his staff."

She exhaled softly, the breath lifting a loose strand of her white-blond hair. "He apologized rather nicely."

"And I didn't?"

Hell. Mitch raked a hand through his hair. Two minutes alone and they were on the brink of another clash. He could all but hear the crackle of tension in the air, and he didn't need to ask if she got his point. The past swirled, dark with shadowy secrets, in her eyes.

"You had no need to apologize." Her voice

sounded about as tight as her pale-knuckled grip on the empty glass. "I told you nothing happened."

"Hell, Emily, you were in my bed, and I can't remember anything after kissing you. If that's all that happened—"

"It is." She put the glass down with a decisive clunk. "You were drunk and grieving and, yes, you kissed me, and we somehow ended up in your bed. You passed out and that's all that happened."

The rushed telling brought a flush to her face, the same sweet, pink color he'd seen all over her body that next morning. "We also, somehow, ended up naked," he pointed out.

The color in her cheeks flared, hotter, darker, but she met his eyes. "You didn't have a clue what you were doing. Or who with."

"I knew who I was with, Emily," he said emphatically. "Now I need to know what I did."

"*Nothing,* Mitch." Temper sparked in her eyes, charging Mitch with the same fiery frustration.

"It's not 'nothing' if it sent you packing and if it's still preventing you taking your job back. Damn it, Emily, I've given you the freedom to name your price and conditions. I've given you thinking time. Joshua loves you and I'm pretty sure you feel the same way. If it's not me—if it's not about that night—then what's the problem?"

With the music suddenly shut down, that last question sounded far too loud, aggressive, abrasive. Obviously, his sister thought so, too, because from beside the stereo she insisted, "Stop bullying her."

"Butt out, Chantal." His focus switched back to Emily, needing *her* response, *her* answer. "Tell me why you won't come and work for me."

"How about because you're obnoxious," Chantal said, putting herself between them, arms folded, expression determined.

"She needs a job, sis."

"We're working on that."

Everything inside him ground to a halt. "Care to explain?"

"Good grief, Mitch, you can't force Emily to work for you. And when she makes up her mind—which won't be with you standing over her—it will be because she has choices. Now, was there anything else you wanted?" his sister, the turncoat, asked sweetly. "Besides the chance to browbeat my houseguest?"

Seething, Mitch gritted his teeth. "If it's still all right with your houseguest, I'd like to buy her grandfather's dog for Joshua."

Through an agency in Cliffton, Mitch found temporary child care in the form of a middle-aged cleanliness guru with the unlikely name of Mrs. Grubb. More interested in keeping the house free of dust and lint than keeping Joshua entertained and happy, she wasn't working out.

As if to punctuate that thought, her vacuum cleaner started up, its high-pitched whine eating through the last of his concentration. *Earmuffs, industrial strength.* He started a mental shopping list, then wondered if Mrs. Grubb did shopping. It would get her out of the house, even if it did defeat the child care purpose of her employment, because he was not, no way, sending Joshua to any shopping center.

The machine's whine intensified as his office door opened, then ebbed as it clicked shut. Joshua rested his chin on the edge of the desk and looked up at him with serious eyes. "Is it 'kay to ask one question?"

"Only one?" Mitch ruffled his hair. "Spit it out, bud."

"Is it time for Digger's walk yet?"

"Not quite." He swung back to the desk and right-clicked on the computer clock. "When the big hand's up here, see? You can check on the kitchen clock. Okay?"

Joshua sighed heavily. "'Kay, Daddy."

That despondent little voice, the sound of his re-treating footsteps, the restrained thud of the closing door—they all combined to knock the stuffing right out of Mitch. A numbing sense of acceptance rose up to fill the void. Emily wasn't changing her mind. For over a week he'd kept his distance, working while he could, making do with this temporary excuse for a nanny, waiting for any sign of Em's attitude mellowing.

It hadn't; it wouldn't. Because no matter how many times she denied it, how many times she used that *nothing* word, she couldn't hide the tumult in her eyes. He had slept with her. He'd shattered her trust in him as a boss and as a man, and his ham-fisted attempt to force the full story from her hadn't done his cause any favors.

He'd blown it.

Now he needed to contact some decent agencies and start the nanny hunt all over again. Since his cur-rent chapter wasn't going anywhere—two pathetic paragraphs since lunch—he clicked online and searched for the Yellow Pages.

Fifteen minutes later he'd set the wheels in motion, but the consequences grated as harshly as the incessant howl of the bloody vacuum cleaner. Another nanny who wasn't Emily. It felt...wrong.

With a soft oath, he spun his chair away from the desk and took his frustration to the kitchen. While he waited for coffee to brew, he grabbed a fruit box from the fridge and went searching for the son who made his world seem more right. The rumpus room was empty and he combed the rest of the house—resisting the impulse to check inside Mrs. Grubb's cleaner— and came up Joshua-less.

Recalling his question about walking Digger, Mitch checked the kitchen clock. Ten to four. His mild irritation morphed to annoyance as he headed outside. Joshua knew he had to ask before going outdoors. It was a rule. But that's where he'd be, playing with his new best friend.

He wasn't in the yard. Worry churning his gut, Mitch strode back inside, flicked the off switch on the machine-from-hell and faced down Mrs. Grubb's indignation. "Have you seen Joshua?"

"Why, he's in the rumpus room, watching tele—"

Mitch didn't wait around. He was back outside, calling out to Joshua, whistling for Digger. Why hadn't he thought of that before? Find the dog and he would find Joshua.

Nothing.

His heart pounded. *Think, Mitch, think.*

Emily. All day Joshua had harped about showing her Digger's latest trick, and that's what the four-o'clock walk was all about. Going to see Emily. His panic steadied. With five, ten minutes head start he'd be still on the road. A quiet road, he reminded the sudden jitter in his pulse. Only local traffic to a handful of farms.

Grabbing his cell phone, he strode to his truck, fired the engine and turned down the drive. The road was empty, no traffic, no boy. Resisting the urge to drive fast, he scanned the roadside thoroughly, across the long-grassed paddocks either side. No fair-haired boy, no dog, no sign of activity except a soaring hawk intent on some ground prey.

Phone in hand, he dialed Chantal's number, impatiently waited six rings before Emily's quiet hello. Thank God, someone was home.

"Is Joshua there?"

A beat of pause. "No. Should he be?"

"He's missing. I thought he headed down to see you. Can you check outside?"

Barely breathing, he awaited her reply, all the while steadily surveying the landscape for any sign of boy or dog. His whole body tightened with expectation, fear, hope when he heard the clunk of the phone being lifted.

"I'm sorry, Mitch. I'll start walking back from my end across the paddocks. Don't worry, that's where he'll be, somewhere between the two houses."

Mitch nodded, unable to speak, unable to see beyond the awful, pounding revisitation of his worst nightmare.

His son was lost.

Four

They tramped the thickly grassed fields between Mitch's and Chantal's homes, calling, whistling, receiving no reply save the distant caw of a lone crow. Emily's stomach churned, sick with panicky fear. The urge to run, to scream Joshua's name, clawed at her composure. Guilt clawed at her conscience.

He'd been bringing Digger to visit. If she'd taken the job, or even taken the time to visit… If she'd not been so selfishly absorbed in her own fears…

"Mitch!"

Startled by that distant call, Emily swung around to see a familiar farm truck barrel to a stop right beside Mitch. Quade swung from the cab, followed by both Anderson brothers from down the road.

One look at the mens' faces shattered her sharp spike of hope. They weren't delivering good news, but they were more than doubling the feet and eyes in the search. Perhaps now the fields would not seem so endless, the horizons so far, night so near. Especially now that real numbers were on the way.

"We should wait here for the Rescue Squad, plan our—"

"You can wait." Mitch interrupted Quade's suggestion, his gaze fixed on the forest to the east. The Tibaroo Nature Reserve. Haven to rabbits and hares and wildlife. Heaven to a terrier-cross with an instinctive nose for pursuit.

Emily's heartbeat skipped. "He can't have gone that far," she murmured, hopeful, hoping.

Mitch didn't answer. He was already striding into the lengthening shadows, toward the eucalypts that loomed tall and dark in the graying light of dusk. Emily rubbed her hands up and down her arms to ward off the sudden chill. How much more menacing they must appear to one small boy.

Alone.

The tide of panic rose again, lapping at her confidence, flooding her senses. Until her gaze fixed on Mitch's broad, straight back. The man with the most at stake still managed to radiate strength and purpose and calm determination.

The panic receded as she released a long pent-up breath and hurried after him. Index fingers to tongue, she whistled the long-two-note, short-note call that Digger recognized. That was her purpose—to find the dog that would lead them to the boy.

"You should wait with the others," Mitch called over his shoulder.

"What others?"

He turned then, narrowed gaze scanning the small search party. The Andersons tracked a wide arc to his left, Quade trod a diagonal path to his right. No one had waited; they had all taken their lead from him. Something flickered in his eyes—recognition? renewed resolve?—then he gave a short, sharp nod and continued.

But when they reached the fence demarking forest from farmland, still with no sign of boy or dog, Quade stopped his brother-in-law with a hand on his shoulder. "The Rescue Squad is five minutes away. They know this place—bushwalkers get lost here every other month. Let them do their job, mate. They'll have searchlights."

As if on cue, the sun commenced its slide behind the hills, signaling the approach of night. Darkness. Fear. A muscle jumped in Mitch's tightly clenched jaw, and when he rested his hands atop the solid timber stile, Emily saw their fine tremor.

Beneath the stoic facade, the determined stride, Mitch Goodwin was terrified.

That knowledge hit hard, winding her for a moment. Her peripheral senses registered the activity around her—Quade cursing the lack of cell phone coverage; the Andersons striding back the way they'd come, waving directions to an approaching truck—while her heart ached to reassure the man at her side, to soothe his anguish.

Mouth dry, heart thumping, she touched a hand to his ramrod-straight back, felt his tension, the jump in his nerves, and had to say something, anything.

"Do you think he would have come this far?"

"If the dog chased a rabbit, if he followed the dog." He shrugged, a short, sharp movement. "Yes."

Her dog. She'd thought him the perfect companion for Joshua, lively and mischievous and adventuresome—if only she'd considered the other side to those qualities. This outcome. Her fault. If they found him…no, *when* they found him, she would make it up to them both.

"We'll find him, Mitch," she whispered.

For a moment he said nothing, just stood there staring into the darkening bush. Then slowly he turned to look right at her. "I shouldn't have lost him. I shouldn't have failed him again."

The haunted pain in his eyes, the bleak bitterness of his voice—she had experienced those before. His failure to save his marriage, to talk his beautiful, runaway wife into returning, had consumed him, Emily knew, but did he feel he'd failed Joshua, too? Because he couldn't salvage his marriage, because he'd struggled with child care arrangements? Because a nanny had lost her headstrong charge in a city mall?

The last time, she had tried to comfort him with words, words that seemed like tired old platitudes. Now only one thing needed saying, one certainty. "You won't fail him, Mitch. You never have."

"You know that for a fact?"

"My heart does," she said simply, holding his gaze, wanting so badly to wrap her arms around him, to hold him, to ease his anguish.

Denial burned in his eyes, but before he could speak, a distant shout broke the intense intimacy that bound them. More voices, then lights crested the hill and cut across the field. Caught in their artificial brilliance, his face looked harsh, his torment so sharply hewn that she started to lift a hand, to reach out, but a flicker of caution in his eyes stopped her.

The searchlight moved on, past them, and he wheeled away, hurdling the stile in one smooth leap.

Emily had only clambered halfway over the rough timber structure before he disappeared around the first curve in the fire trail that snaked into the trees.

"Mitch. Wait up!"

Heart pounding, she raced after him, wide eyes scanning the ground for branches or exposed roots that might trip her up. Ahead she heard the occasional crack of a twig beneath his boots or caught a glimpse of his pale-blue sweater between the dark columns of stringy ironbark. She thanked the Lord he wasn't wearing his dark coat.

Fifty yards farther she wished her heavy, constricting coat to perdition. She paused, lifted her fingers to her lips, but needed to quiet her labored breathing before she could whistle effectively. Then she trudged on at a slow jog, determined to catch up with him, surprising herself by doing so around the next curve in the trail. Stock-still, he stood straight and tall, listening.

"Did you hear something?"

"Shhh," he cautioned, a hand on her sleeve. Then his eyes narrowed. "Hear that?"

All senses straining, she listened, one pounding beat of her heart, two…then she heard it, somewhere to their right. A low, whimpering sound, almost as soft as the darkness. Mitch's grip on her sleeve tightened for a millisecond—the time it took him to breathe "Joshua"—and then he ploughed into the undergrowth like some human bulldozer.

Emily wavered. Should she race back for the others or follow him? One sharp yap—absolutely Digger—sent her crashing into the bush in Mitch's wake. Thick, hot tears of blessed relief blurred her vision, and she tripped over a log, felt herself falling and grabbed for the spindly branches of a low-growing shrub. Needle-sharp spines bit into her palms and a loose branch lashed her throat as she went down in a heap. Around her the silence seemed eerily complete.

"Mitch?" she called, her voice rising on a slight note of panic.

"Over here."

Clambering to her feet, she saw him ahead, off to her right.

"We're both over here."

At first she wondered if she'd misunderstood that simple pronouncement, but when she hunkered down in front of Mitch she realized that father and son were bound so closely in each other's arms that she'd missed the small body. The pain of relief ached in her chest, the effort of holding back her dammed-up tears scalded her throat.

At her feet Digger whined, a low, keening call for sympathy, and Mitch opened his eyes. They appeared uncannily dark, still haunted, still pained. One large hand was splayed against his son's fair head, holding him tightly against his chest as if he might never let him go.

"Is he all right?" she managed to mouth.

Mitch nodded. Then he released a long whoosh of residual tension and fear. "Thank you, God."

He allowed Joshua to cling a moment longer, then eased him back enough that he could look into his face.

"You're just fine, aren't you, bud?"

Joshua scrubbed a fisted hand across his face and sniffed loudly. Then his small face crumpled and he burrowed back against his father's broad chest.

The expression on Mitch's face shifted. A new determination sculpted his mouth in a firm line. The stubbornness in his jaw intensified, fire burned in the depths of his dark eyes as they met Emily's. "You'll start Monday."

He didn't ask, he stated the bald fact, and Emily didn't say a word. Didn't even nod. She knew the answer was written all over her face, had been ever since Joshua went missing. She would start right now if that's what he wanted, but Monday gave her two days to steel herself. Two short days when six months hadn't been nearly enough.

Heaven help her.

The next day Mitch learned that nothing with this new, quixotic Emily was that easy…not with his little sister, the champion negotiator, in her corner. Yes, she would start on Monday, but on a trial basis.

"And if this trial fails?" he'd asked.

"I won't leave you in the lurch. I'll stay until you finish your book or find a suitable replacement." Which sounded fair enough, except her cool, uptight tone reeked of Chantal's coaching—how else could she have known he was writing a book?—and he couldn't stop himself retorting in a similar tone.

Less than two minutes later the employment negotiations had lapsed into a ridiculous game of one-upmanship. He insisted she live in. She chose the smallest, least comfortable of the three unoccupied bedrooms. Since it was the farthest from his, Mitch gritted his teeth and let it be…after informing her that he would be teaching her to drive.

Ten days later, as he prowled the verandah in a restless after-midnight ritual, he could still see the fiery spark in her eyes as she swung around to deliver her comeback. And as for the comeback itself…he shook his head, remembering: "Fine. You can *try* and teach me to drive providing you forget about what happened that night. No more questions, no more demands."

What the hell possessed him to agree? Sure, he'd been caught off guard by her audacious demand. He'd laughed at its twisted irony—she wanted him to "forget" a night he didn't, largely, remember.

"No worries," he'd drawled while her eyes clouded with skepticism. She knew his need-to-know nature needed to know, even if she didn't understand how much that night plagued his mind and body. But that wariness in her eyes…*that* had kept him to his promise these past ten days. Hands on hips, he stopped pacing and blew out a ragged breath.

Hell, some of those days he'd ached with the effort of "forgetting," although mostly it wasn't so difficult—they had the perfect, ever-present chaperone in Joshua with his games and television and chatter. But then a seemingly casual remark would resonate with hidden meaning or a casual brushing of limbs or the scent of her freshly bathed skin would catapult him to a different level of awareness: Emily, the woman.

In his house, naked in his shower, asleep between her pristine sheets in the bedroom down the hall.

Sucking in a breath, he felt the bite of winter air in his nostrils, in his lungs, sharp with the edge of citrus but not nearly sharp enough to shut out the hot ache of sexual frustration. His constant companion. Before he started howling at the moon, he hurdled the verandah rail and cut across the lawn. A long hike through the brittle, winter night might not cool his blood, but it would clear his head enough to remember his final rejoinder in that negotiation battle.

"No worries," he'd drawled as her eyes clouded with skepticism. "Seeing as this is a business relationship and I have a duty of care as your employer, it wouldn't be appropriate to ever mention you'd been in my bed. Would it?"

Forty-five minutes later the glow of light caught his attention as he crested the last rolling rise and the old homestead came into view. A punch of fear, low in his gut, set him running flat out.

Sitting room window, he told himself. No need to overreact. She likely couldn't sleep.

Mitch forced himself to get a grip—he didn't want to scare the bejesus out of Emily by bursting into the house like a madman—but he could have saved himself the effort of slowing down. In the empty room a circular pool of lamplight revealed a magazine set aside and a glass on the side table. The rest of the house sat in darkness, enveloped in the heavy silence of sleep.

"Emily?"

Pausing outside her bedroom, he tapped lightly on the door, willing her to answer. He sure as hell did not want to open that door, to see her in her bed, to carry that image—

"Mitch."

At the soft sound of his name, he whirled around, saw her three doors down—outside Joshua's room—and was beside her in less than a second.

"Is he all right? What's happened?"

With a finger to her lips, she shushed his questions. "Bad dream," she whispered. "But he's gone back to sleep."

Mitch needed to see for himself. In the shadows of the night-light Joshua slept soundly, his fair hair mussed as if by her hand. Both arms hugged a teddy bear he'd never seen before. A scruffy bear, he noticed as he bent down to kiss his son's brow, its shaggy coat threadbare in places, battle-scarred in others, probably from years gripped in small arms. Including Emily's?

He straightened and met her eyes. ''Looks like your bear's been through the wars.''

''That's his job,'' she said with soft sincerity. ''Fighting night-fear battles.''

For a second Mitch stood speechless, blown away, and then he shook his head. Of course Emily would produce the perfect solution for Joshua's night fears— not just a comforting companion, but one who fought the demons and bore the battle scars to prove it.

''Does he have a name?'' he asked, guiding her from the room.

''Bruiser.'' The hint of a smile touched her lips as she pulled the door to behind them. ''Thus dubbed around fifteen minutes ago. I thought it suited a lean, mean fighting machine better than his previous Bruce name.''

In the hallway he turned her around to face him, but dropped his hands when her eyes widened warily. ''Was he frightened?''

''Disoriented mostly.''

''It's been a lot for him to deal with, all the changes, even before that latest misadventure.''

She bit her lip, then pushed a long tress of silvery hair back over her shoulder with one hand, revealing a tangible reminder of that misadventure. A scratch from the spiky undergrowth traced the line of her throat and disappeared beneath the neckline of her thick robe.

Mitch had seen the mark most every day, along with shallower, now-healed pricks on her hands. But prior knowledge did not stop the violent jolt of reaction deep in his gut—every day—or the sudden itch to lift his hand and trace the scar its full length.

He shoved both hands in his pockets, away from temptation, and noticed her fidgety shift of weight from one foot to the other. Nervous. Of standing here with him in the near darkness? Given the itch in his fingers, she had cause.

"He used to wake often," he said quietly, forcing himself to relax against the wall at her side and hoping she might do the same. Relax for a while, forget their tensions and his rogue intentions. "He went through a stage of bad dreams, crying in his sleep, clinging."

"Afraid you might leave, too."

Yeah, Emily *would* understand. She'd been in that same place, shifted and shuffled around right through her childhood, and it made her own flight from his apartment that much harder to understand. But he'd promised not to bring it up, not to question, and that agreement was eating holes in his psyche. He buried his hands deeper in his pockets and cleared his throat. "Thank you for being here, for tonight."

Being Emily, she shifted uncomfortably, a little hitch of one shoulder, and he felt the brush of her robe against his sleeve and hip, felt a reactive warmth wash through him.

"Well, night fears are my specialty," she said finally, and although she dipped her head so her hair slid forward to obscure her face, he pictured a wry half smile on her lips. He liked the image, liked the new teasing tone.

"Yeah?" Leaning closer, he nudged her with his shoulder. "You have another lean, mean, fighting-machine bear for *my* night fears?"

With one finger she slowly threaded that silky fall of hair back behind her ear. In the shadows her eyes looked dark and troubled.

Night fears are my specialty. Damn.

Already he could sense her withdrawal, and he struggled for a way to wipe that contrite why-did-he-say-that expression from her face. To keep her here in the dark, talking, almost companionable.

"Were you having trouble sleeping?" he asked, remembering the scene in the sitting room. "It looked like you'd been up reading, before Joshua woke."

"I was watching television, actually." She darted him an edgy look. "I hope you don't mind."

"Why would I mind?"

"I know you work some nights." She paused, seemingly intent on studying her toes. Bare, he noticed, nails painted a pearly pink that reminded him of her bare skin. "I didn't want to disturb you."

"Hell, Emily, your being here dis—" He cut himself off abruptly. Still thinking about her bare skin, he'd almost revealed that her very presence disturbed him, asleep or awake, that even the sight of her bare toes turned him on. He expelled a harsh breath before trying again. "It's not you that's disrupting my writing."

Head bowed, face hidden, she didn't reply. He lifted a hand, intent on tucking her hair back, but at his touch she jolted upright, and the sleek strands slid over his wrist, shockingly cool, seductively soft.

"I should go back to bed," she said in a breathy rush.

And he should let her, except—damn it—he didn't want her gone. He wanted to preserve this mood, this strange edgy intimacy. He'd avoided being alone with her, and now he needed her company. Not quite the old Emily with her quiet, easy manner, but still easy to talk to, to be with....

He straightened off the wall and took a gamble on the changed Emily. "Don't you want to satisfy your curiosity?"

Wariness darkened her shadowy eyes...wariness *and* a puzzled sense of curiosity.

Mitch smiled with no small measure of satisfaction. Then winked. "Join me in the kitchen for hot chocolate, and I'll tell you what it is you're curious about."

Five

After the concentrated, darkened intimacy of the hall-way, Emily found some respite in the brightly lit kitchen and the fact that Mitch was now one island bench and half a room away. Seated on a stool at said bench, she watched him with a fascination that totally eclipsed her curiosity.

He moved with such economy—an almost fluid grace that elevated the mundane art of hot-chocolate preparation to an artistic plane. A thing of beauty. The way his long fingers embraced the mugs, the smooth shoulder-nudge that closed the pantry door, the intense focus on his face as he measured out the powdered chocolate. Heck, she even loved the way his sweater shifted with the play of muscles in his shoulders and back.

Her gaze continued down. Jeans, not too tight—and she wasn't allowing herself to look too hard, uh-

uh—and his old walking shoes. *Walking?* She sat up straighter on the stool. Now she was totally busting with curiosity.

"Were you out walking?"

Obviously surprised, he cut her a quick glance, his eyes glittering gray-green in the fluorescent light.

"You would have heard Joshua, from your office, if that's where you were. I just realized," she finished lamely as the microwave peeped. *Bingo. You've got it.*

He poured the hot milk before he looked up again. "Yeah, I was taking a walk."

"At 2:00 a.m.?"

With a lopsided grin—the one that always caused Emily's heart to loop the loop—he deposited the filled mugs on the bench. "But that's not what you're curious about."

Emily blinked. "It's not?"

"You want to know what's disrupting my writing."

Yup, she *was* curious about that comment. Turning superciliously, she tilted her head so she could watch him stroll around the bench. *He's going to sit next to me.* Her heart skipped a beat, restarted with a new vigor. *Goodbye respite.*

When he slid onto the stool next to hers, their knees bumped. Emily steeled herself not to jump, wriggle or fan the sudden heat that suffused her body and crept into her face. *Act cool, Emily Jane. Cool, yet friendly.* Because this night, this sharing, constituted a quantum leap in their…relationship. For want of a better word.

"Is this your foreign correspondent book?"

Mug halfway to his mouth, he paused and stared.

"Chantal mentioned it," she admitted. Then, when he continued to stare— "We weren't talking about you or anything. She was telling Quade, and I happened to overhear. It will be a fabulous book, Mitch."

"Yeah, well, it's not looking so fabulous from this side of the pages."

"Why ever not?" She knew the work he'd done in the field, the awards he'd won, before taking a studio job with fixed hours. Because he'd wanted to save his marriage. Right now he was frowning into his hot chocolate. "You must have so much material."

"Lack of material isn't a problem. It's getting it all together, how I want it, and making the publisher's deadline."

"What happens if you don't?"

His eyes snapped up. "That's not an option."

"Because you have a contract?"

"Yes."

Emily frowned at the vehemence of his answer, not understanding. "If you need the money so badly, why were you threatening to throw houses and cars my way?"

"It's not the money, Em." Determination burned in his eyes. "It's about doing what I said I'd do, about honoring that commitment, about getting this one thing in my life right."

Ahh. Understanding beckoned, like a glimmer of light beneath a lifting fog. Carefully she put down her drink. He believed he'd failed as a husband, as a father, as her employer. Mitch Goodwin who didn't have a clue how to handle failure because he'd always known nothing but success. Emily didn't know whether to hug him or shake him.

"Don't you think," she began carefully, "that a book you're not happy with would be a worse kind of failure? Like failing yourself and your standards?"

"Yeah, and that thought's not helping the block."

"Maybe you need to cut yourself some slack."

"Maybe I need to sort out the other stuff in my life so I can focus on the book." With a rough bark of laughter, he dragged his fingers through his hair, shook his head. "Which you've already done, with Joshua, with the whole household organization thing."

Absurdly flattered, she couldn't help smiling. "Along with night fears, sorting stuff is one of my specialties. What else needs sorting?"

Heat sparked in his eyes, sudden and startling. Emily's stomach tightened. Her pulse quickened. But then he looked away, studied his mug for a long second, and she didn't know whether to be relieved that he'd reined in that random thought or disappointed. "Annabelle's parents contacted me, about Joshua," he said finally. "Through their lawyer."

Emily gaped. "Surely they're not contesting custody?"

"They want regular visitation."

Oh. Emily traced a slow finger around the rim of her mug, and when she looked up he was eyeing her narrowly. "You don't have an opinion?"

"Well, yes," Emily said cautiously, "but it may not be the one you want to hear."

One corner of his mouth twisted, but he made a give-it-to-me gesture with one hand.

"Well, I think they have a right and so does Joshua. I know what it's like not to have family contact, and if I knew that was because someone blocked the process…'' What would she do? A hypothetical she didn't bother answering because the only thing that stopped her parents from visits was their own lack of parental affection. Luckily she'd had her Gramps. ''Keeping grandparents from seeing their grandchild is wrong, Mitch.''

''I'm not stopping them,'' he said tersely. ''All they need to do is pick up the phone, personally, not through a law office.''

''Have you picked up the phone, Mitch?'' No, she could see the answer in his expression and she shook her head. ''You always used to be the first to take a step like that, to make things happen.''

Grim-faced, he looked away. ''Yeah, I used to do a lot of things. Past tense.''

Used to, before Annabelle left. An old resentment sliced through Emily, one she hadn't allowed herself to acknowledge in a long, long time. A sharp, bitter antipathy toward the woman whose memory stopped him from doing those things. The ex-wife who had taken and taken and tossed it all back in his face. And, worse, deeper, sharper, flared her anger at Mitch for being too stubborn or, yes, probably still hurting too much, to move forward. To do a simple little thing such as holding out a conciliatory hand to Joshua's grandparents.

''Maybe it's time you stopped blaming yourself for what happened,'' she said, her voice stronger, more strident than she'd intended. ''The Blaineys have been hurting—are still hurting—just as much as you. Make it easy on them and Joshua and yourself. Call them.''

''Blaineys' Snowhawk Lodge.'' Mitch stared at the Yellow Pages listing on his monitor. There. He had the number, his last excuse nixed. All he had to do was dial, make the arrangements. Maybe he wouldn't even have to meet with them and see the grief in their eyes, the condemnation, the disappointment. He hadn't been able to make her happy or even keep her content, their precious only daughter, and God knows he had tried. Right up until the end.

Pick up the phone, make the call. If not for Joshua, or his ex-in-laws, he needed to do it for himself, anything to erase the memory of Emily's expression as she told him—basically—to get over himself. He had always valued her opinion, had hated her recent circumspection around him, but last night he'd discovered something that struck much deeper. Emily Warner's disappointment. Something else to keep him awake nights.

With a disgusted snort, he rocked forward in his chair and reached for the phone...just as his screensaver activated, obliterating the number. Before he could do more than curse, once, succinctly, he heard activity outside. Voices, indistinct, indiscernible. A door opening and closing. He didn't hear footsteps in the carpeted hallway but sensed them, and he counted the seconds until his office door swung open. First guess: his little sister.

"Ah, the writer hermit in his cave."

Yup, Chantal, wearing a maternity tent and a worried scowl.

"Why don't you come in, sis." He scowled right back at her as she plopped down in the office's second chair. "And make yourself at home."

"I would if you had some decent furniture in here. This chair is the pits."

Exactly. Visitor discouragement. He gestured at this visitor's heavily pregnant belly. "Did you waddle down here or drive?"

"I wish! Waddling from one room to the next is my limit, and I don't fit behind the wheel anymore. Quade drove me. He's somewhere out there." A casual wave indicated the garden beyond his window. "Practicing his daddy skills on Joshua."

Banished so his wife could practice her nagging skills on him. Wonderful. Mitch set his expression to implacable and rocked back in his own very comfortable chair.

"We've been to Cliffton for my checkup and decided to drop in on our way past. Seeing as you *never* bother returning my calls. And, yes, I am well, thanks for asking."

"Emily keeps me informed."

"So, you do come out of the cave occasionally?"

He bared his teeth. "Only to feed."

Chantal didn't even roll her eyes let alone laugh. Obviously she was more pissed off than he'd thought. "That would be the food Emily prepares, I presume?"

"Your point?"

"My point?" Swift fury flared in her eyes. "When did Emily last have a meal cooked for her. Or a night off?"

Mitch bridled. "She has Sundays off. I offered more—"

"So she could sit in her room? Or maybe *walk* the twelve miles to town?"

The driving lessons. *That's* what this was about.

"You haven't even started yet, have you? Dammit, Mitch, you said you would teach her!"

Jaw clenched, he rose to his feet and stared out the window. Yes, he'd said he would teach her, and he intended to keep his word, except he'd been busy. Preoccupied with the book's lack of progress, with the Blaineys, with last-minute changes to his scripts for a documentary series going into production next month.

"Do you remember the summer you tried to teach me to play golf?" his little sister asked.

"How could I forget? You sucked."

"No, *you* sucked. Big-time." He heard her getting to her feet—it took a while—then he felt her hand on his shoulder. "Let Quade teach her, Mitch. He has the time, he's patient. And he's a good communicator."

"I said I'd do it and I will."

"Stubborn ass."

But the insult came coated in a smile, a smile that wiped the scorn from her eyes and softened her expression. Probably because, through his office window, she watched her patient husband playing ball with his son and communicating with his nanny. Making her laugh. Something in his gut wound tight. Something that had nothing to do with stubborn.

"I'll teach Emily to drive," he said. "You need Quade at home."

"Because of jelly bean?" She touched a hand to her belly. "My doctor says I have another month to go. Unfortunately."

"Julia's doctor said she had another month to go." And their sister had scared the stuffing out of them all with her early, emergency dash to the maternity ward. Beside him Chantal shifted restlessly, maybe remembering, maybe worrying, and he looped an arm around her shoulders, reminding her that family would be there for her, too. "You'll do fine, sis."

"I know."

In silence they observed the game unfolding outside. Quade had turned football coach, kicking to Joshua who caught the high ball, evaded a feeble attempt at a tackle from Emily and steamed toward the try line. Mitch nudged his sister. "Did you see that take? Like father, like son."

Chantal snorted, distracted as he'd intended. She slanted him a look. "How is he doing?"

"You have to ask? Look at him."

And they did, saw his serious little face as he tried to teach Emily how to kick the football. She tried, she failed, she shrugged and passed the ball back to the four-year-old expert whose chest puffed with self-importance.

"That's the magic of Emily," he said quietly.

"The perfect nanny." Her pause seemed measured. Or careful. "Has she said anything more about leaving?"

Leaving. The word was a sick, scary feeling in his gut, a fist clenching his throat. Still he managed to ask, "To you?"

"No. But I did promise to keep my ear out for jobs, and yesterday I heard about a lawyer who's looking for—"

"Don't even think about telling Emily," he ground out. Then, "I need her to stay, sis."

"For how long? Indefinitely?"

"Preferably, yes."

Chantal eyed him narrowly, as if trying to decide

if he was joking or for real. Then she gave a short, strangled laugh. "Then perhaps you should marry her."

Chantal's visit completely shot his working day. After she left—after she deliberately sought out Emily for a none-too-brief and private consultation—he couldn't even stare at the walls in peace. Now he walked the office, wall to wall and back again, his temper sparking.

She wasn't leaving; he wouldn't allow it.

And how will you stop her? Bolt the doors, padlock the gates, impound the car keys? The irony of the last option brought his pacing up short. He rubbed at the tension knot in the back of his neck. So, okay, honesty time. He hadn't avoided driving lessons for lack of time or opportunity. He'd been avoiding the closeted closeness of a vehicle, one-on-one, until his libido settled down.

Some time next century.

Just thinking about their last encounter, not an hour ago, ignited his blood all over again. After waving Quade and Chantal goodbye, Joshua dragged them both into the sitting room to watch *Blues Clues*. Somehow a tickling game got out of hand and his hands got on Emily, and the silliness turned sultry when she stopped squirming and he looked into her eyes.

Awareness arced between them, immediate and electric. His hands tightened on her waist and under her soft flannel shirt he imagined her bare skin, milk pale, satin smooth. Her mouth had softened, her lips parted, he'd caught a glimpse of her small, pink tongue. Mitch groaned, remembering. If they hadn't been on the sitting room floor in broad daylight, if

Joshua hadn't bounced back into the room with the toy he'd run to fetch...

And he was expected to lock himself inside a car with her? For an hour or more?

Yes. He'd given his word; he had to do it. And he had to keep his hands to himself. She was his nanny, his employee, and his thoughts alone would send her packing.

Perhaps you should marry her.

Earlier he'd laughed dismissively at Chantal's tongue-in-cheek suggestion, but he wasn't laughing now. The perfect nanny, the perfect stepmother for Joshua. The perfect wife? Mitch's heart knocked against his ribs, the rhythm a powerful mix of hope and deep-seated terror.

He'd married Annabelle in haste, because he'd wanted her, because she thought she'd wanted him. When the haze of lust lifted, he'd found himself married to a woman he didn't really know—a *pregnant* woman he didn't really know—let alone like. If he were to marry again, it would be for practical reasons, and six months ago Emily would have topped his list of perfect, practical candidates. Her even temperament, her empathic insights, her warm, quiet presence in his home every day.

Her lush body in his bed every night.

No. That particular part of his body wasn't motivating any marriage decision, not ever again. He huffed out a hot, wry breath. *Any marriage decision.* What was he thinking? It had taken three weeks and a lost child to convince Emily to come work for him—to trial him as a boss, for cripe's sake!—so why would she consider marrying him?

What could he offer?

Not a damn thing he could think of, but he could at least keep his promise regarding her terms of employment. Keys in hand, he strode out to the sitting room and stuck his head through the doorway.

"Who wants to go get ice cream?"

"In town?" Joshua bounded to his feet. "Me, me, meeee!"

Predictable. Mitch's gaze shifted to Emily…Emily shaking her head. "I think I'll pass."

"Uh-uh. You don't get to pass." Mitch tossed the keys in the air and caught them again with a decisive snatch of the hand. "It's time for your first driving lesson."

An argument wasn't the best way to start a lesson, Emily knew, but she couldn't help objecting. Forget the fact that the word *driving* made her as nervous as a pigeon in a cathouse. Forget the added stress of *him* sitting beside her, issuing tight-lipped instructions. She simply couldn't handle the size or manual transmission of his tank of a truck. Which didn't stop Mitch insisting she could.

After kangaroo-hopping down the drive until the engine stalled—for the third time—she turned to him, teeth set. "I told you I couldn't do this."

"And I told you we'd keep trying until you could. Today Joshua only wants ice cream. Next week it could be medicine. Now, clutch in—"

"Look, Mitch, I can barely see over the wheel. It's dangerous." She flicked a telling glance at the rear-view mirror, at the precious cargo strapped into the car seat of the crew cab, oblivious to the tension up front. "Think about it."

He caught her point and considered it for all of, oh, two seconds. "Fine. I'll drive."

Relief washed through her, so liberating she actually slouched over the wheel. "Thank you," she whispered.

"We'll borrow Julia's car for lessons until I can buy you something suitable."

She straightened abruptly. "I told you before, I don't want you buying me a car."

"I wouldn't be buying it for you. I'd be buying it for Joshua, for his care and security."

Okay. She could concede that point, for now, although the uncompromising set of his jaw did not bode well for future discussions on the matter. Or for a nice, relaxed afternoon drive, she added as he curtly suggested they change seats. Perhaps after the ice cream break his mood would mellow.

It didn't. In fact, after ice cream things got worse.

First, Julia decided Joshua should stay with her, to help with Bridie. At nine months, Bridie was a bundle of chortling mischief even Joshua could not ignore. He agreed she needed some guy company...as long as he didn't have to change diapers. Emily felt a sense of doom enfold her in a blanket of gray, as heavy and ominous as the winter sky above. Then Julia handed over the keys to her compact sedan, and she started to sweat.

Fifteen point four-five fraught minutes after clearing the town's derestriction signs, the rain started. Not driving torrents that defied the efforts of windshield wipers and forced drivers to pull over and wait it out, but a gentle misting drizzle.

"Wipers," Mitch directed.

Until this moment she'd been so intensely focused

on performing the mechanics of foot and hand and eye coordination—never her strong point—that she'd paid little attention to the conditions. The prospect of rain. She wet her dry lips and attempted to prise her fingers from the steering wheel. Failed. "I can't," she croaked.

"What do you mean, you can't?"

When she didn't answer—what could she say, that her fingers seemed stuck to the wheel?—he reached across and flicked the switch himself.

"There's a lay-by a few hundred yards ahead," he said tersely. "Pull in there."

Absolutely. I can manage that.

Amazingly she also managed to unpeel her hands from their death grip. An inordinate sense of satisfaction started to well up inside her, and she closed her eyes, overcome, overwhelmed. She drew a long, sustaining breath and found it filled with the clean scent of rain…and man.

Her nerves fluttered back to life. They were alone. Cocooned in a car that suddenly felt way smaller than it looked. Isolated by the blanket of softly falling rain. Alone…until panic crept out of the darkness. It closed in around her, her dark, unwelcome friend, stealing her breath and her reason.

As if from an immense distance she heard movement, the click of a seat belt, the creak of upholstery, and she saw a hand reaching toward her, just like the other time. Without thought, without logic or purpose, she reached for her door handle and bolted.

Six

From inside the car, the rain had appeared deceptively gentle. Outside, Emily hadn't taken a dozen steps before feeling its cold, soaking impact. A half dozen more and it dampened her crazy, panicked flight impulse. Where was she going, anyway? They'd pulled up beside a quiet rural road with nothing in sight save a rickety three-wire fence and, beyond it, a stand of straggly eucalypts with several drenched sheep camped under their questionable shelter…until the slam of a car door sent them scuttling.

Looking back, she saw a darkly glowering Mitch across the rain-slicked roof of the little sedan. No wonder the sheep had run away. "Get back in the car," he barked.

"No." She tossed her head, for emphasis and to remove a hank of wet hair from her face. Even to herself, her refusal seemed as childish and pointless as leaving the car in the first place, yet the prospect of facing Mitch's inevitable inquisition…no way.

"I remember you telling me once how much trouble you have saying that word. No." Eyes never leaving hers, he started around the car. "How you were afraid of earning your parents' displeasure so you always agreed. Miss Compliance, you called yourself."

Emily fought the urge to back up, to turn and flee.

"You want to tell me what's changed?" he asked.

Apparently nothing, because despite the stridency of her *no,* despite her desire to act stronger, to stop giving in to moments of weakness, she'd jumped out of that car. And now she watched his steady, purposeful approach and a frisson of déjà vu—that night he tracked her across Gramps's verandah—sent her spinning around and setting off down the roadside. She heard his muttered reproach, then the heavy squelch of his boots on the wet ground as he strode after her. Felt the steel of his grip as he grabbed her arm and whirled her around.

"What's going on, Emily?"

"I had to get out," she began, "out of the car."

"Claustrophobia?"

She shook her head.

"What, then? You suddenly felt like taking a walk?"

To escape the chill in that narrow, dark glare she closed her eyes, but he pulled her close and a tiny shiver rippled through her skin. Not the cold, she knew, but awareness of his hard heat, his scent, the resonance of his voice as he explained in a low, taut voice that even Joshua knew to keep out of the rain.

The subtext of that message arrested her response midshiver. He thought her a child, a particularly inept child in need of his protective care. That cruel truth should have stopped hurting months ago, yet the barb still stung deep. "I'm not a child, Mitch. And I can tell you right now that a walk in a cyclone holds more appeal than getting back in that car."

"Did the rain spook you? Because you were doing fine before you needed the wipers." Dark brows drawn together, he flipped to journalist mode, piecing his story together. "Was it raining when you had your accident?"

Her gaze shifted, uneasy. A dead giveaway.

"What happened, Em?"

Both hands clasped her upper arms, firm and resolute and warm despite the rain, and Emily inhaled a quick breath. Then she looked into his eyes and released that air on a slow sigh. He wasn't letting her go until she answered. To his satisfaction. "I was carjacked, okay? It was night and, yes, it was raining and in the city and sometimes those triggers freak me out so much I can barely breathe let alone think straight."

The explanation tumbled out, one word on top of the next, and, when her voice hitched at the end, Mitch's hold on her arms gentled. The slightest of movements up and down managed to infiltrate her layers of clothing—managed to feel almost like a caress. The rain and the cold and the atmosphere all seemed to ease, as well. Like a hitch in time.

"When did this happen?" he asked.

"After I left you...your apartment...I got a job nannying for some doctors in Sydney, and this night, my night off, I was going to the movies. In the city." A tremor shivered through her body. "Anyway, after that happened, I couldn't keep the job. They had three kids and a lot of sports and stuff to get to. I came back to Plenty. Gramps's things had to be packed up."

And she didn't have anywhere else to go. For a long moment Mitch couldn't respond, couldn't think under the pounding weight of a dozen conflicting emotions. He focused on the fiercest—the one demanding he find this creep and tear him limb from limb. Jaw clenched, he forced out one question. "Did he hurt you?"

"No. He threatened me and he scared me half to death, but he pushed me out and—"

When she winced, he realized that his redoubled hold on her arms was hurting, but damn it— *"He pushed you out of the car?* And you let us believe you'd had some standard traffic accident? Hell, Emily."

Under his hands he felt her tense and forced himself to ease off, to soothe any damage by rubbing his hands over her arms, her shoulders, her arms again, while fury and protectiveness and frustration and anger played war games in his gut.

"Why didn't you say anything?"

"I'd lost my grandfather and then my share of his will. My home. My pride. Don't you think I felt enough of a victim without sharing this low point, as well?"

"We could have helped—"

"How?" she almost spat back, her forcefulness so unlike Emily that it set him back on his heels. She took the opportunity to twist free, to stand there rubbing her arms as if to rid them of his touch.

Bad move, Emily, he thought, temper crackling. "For a start, I wouldn't have been in the passenger seat for your first driving lesson.'' Barking out orders. Chantal or Julia—*any* woman—should have been doing the teaching. ''And I sure and certain wouldn't have made you drive in the rain.''

Same as he shouldn't be letting her stand in the rain. On the road a farm truck slowed as if preparing to stop, and Mitch waved it on, then shook his head at the absurdity of their situation. Why were they having this discussion on the side of the road in the rain? He made a decision, didn't ask permission. Moving swiftly, he picked her up and started for the car before she could do more than drop her jaw in outrage.

Halfway there, she started to struggle. He ignored her as best he could, given the way her wriggling meant holding her more firmly. Given the fact they were both wet, clothes clinging, her soft curves molded against his hard torso. One part instantly grew harder, but he didn't give a damn. He had other things to contend with...such as opening the car door.

''Put. Me. Down.''

He obliged, sliding her to the ground and trapping her still-wriggling body against the car. But when he dipped down and reached around in a blind search for the door handle, she drew an audible breath and went very still. Because he was touching her? Because that contact sizzled and steamed? Because her jacket had come undone and her shirt was very, very wet? He sucked in a breath.

Little Emily Warner wasn't so little.

Light-headed, he straightened and leaned back and deliberately fastened his gaze on her face. No lower. Jeweled raindrops clung to her skin and her eyelashes, and he felt an insane compulsion to lean forward and lick them away. Tenderness and fierce, throbbing de-

sire blurred into one slow roll of want. He touched a
hand to her face, thumbed away the wetness along
one cheekbone. "You look like a half-drowned kitten," he said thickly.

Against him, beneath him, her whole body stiffened. Her eyes narrowed and for a second he expected
her to hiss like a cornered cat. But she spoke in clear,
strong, defiant syllables. "Let me go, Mitch."

He might have listened, obeyed, if he hadn't seen
the fine flutter of her pulse. If his own fierce ache
hadn't howled in response. Instead he kissed her. The
second his mouth closed over hers, as he felt the
warm expulsion of her surprised breath and the coolness of her rain-slick lips, a tiny *What am I doing?*
alarm went off in his brain.

But the first shy stroke of her tongue against his
bottom lip flipped that alarm switch off. His brain
shut down and his body took over, sinking into her
heat, tongue against tongue, savoring her sweet taste
as the cold turned to fire. Everywhere they touched
burned, and Mitch battled a raging need to fill his
hands with every one of her hot curves. To rip away
clothes and taste her rain-wet skin in a dozen different
places. Right now. Against his sister's car, on the side
of a public road. In timely punctuation, a passing vehicle honked its horn.

Hard.

Breathing heavily, he tore his mouth from hers.
"That wasn't supposed to happen," he said stupidly,
unnecessarily, splaying both hands against the car
roof and letting the shock of cold metal seep into his
heated skin. Steel hard, like him. With a grimace he
pushed himself upright, and, when he saw her face,
his gut twisted, too.

She avoided eye contact, but then she seemed at a loss as to where she *could* look. Her gaze skittered down his body, and heat bloomed in her cheeks. Hard not to notice what was going on down there, especially since they'd been standing hip to hip, and he silently cursed the wet jeans that made his situation even more uncomfortable. And whilst he was in the cursing mood, he flayed whatever impulse let him kiss her, let him threaten the fragile tenure of her employment.

Way to go with the business relationship, Mitch. Very professional.

This was exactly what he'd feared would happen, and he didn't have a clue what to say in explanation. To ensure she didn't leave, again. He exhaled a hot breath and set his jaw. Two things he did know—he needed physical distance to think it through, and he needed to get them both out of this weather.

''Now,'' he asked, ''will you please get in the car?''

Sitting huddled beneath the picnic rug Mitch had found in the trunk, dying a little more with each awkward, passing mile, Emily wished she'd refused that last plea. She could have walked back to town… except walking involved thighs and knees and muscles that no longer worked. Reduced to mush by a kiss he didn't seem in any rush to discuss, debate or dissect.

So far he'd asked if she was comfortable; she said she was fine, thank you. He asked if she wanted the heater turned up; she said no, but could she have the radio? Afternoon talkback droned from the speakers, white noise, along with the rhythmic shwoosh of wiper blades and the sluice of tires through the water sheeting the bitumen. None of which did a blessed thing to silence the questions screaming in her head.

He said she looked like a half-drowned kitten, so why the heck had he kissed her? She didn't think he had a cat fetish. The last time grief and alcohol had provided the kindling, but this time—

"I'm thinking of going to Sydney this week," he said suddenly. "To talk to TVTWO about this documentary series. Is that a problem?"

"You going away?" Emily almost laughed out loud. If being with him was going to be this awkward, strained, unbearable, then... "No. Absolutely not."

"It might be a good idea if we book you some lessons with a professional driving school. A female teacher." He cast a guarded sideways glance. "Chantal said I'd make a lousy teacher."

What could she say to that? I'm not the best judge? Or the ideal pupil? That being in the same space as you creates this incredible awareness that slakes my strength and my good sense?

"I'll look into it when I get back." This time his eyes held hers a moment, until he saw her nod of acquiescence, before returning to the road. "I want you and Joshua to stay with Chantal—"

"Why ever for?" Instantly defensive, she sat up straight.

"I don't think you should be alone in the house."

"I'm quite used to looking after myself. I don't need a sitter." When his jaw clenched—of course he'd disagree!—she tried another angle. "Joshua is settling in really well. It would be stupid to upset his routine. Besides, if we need anything, Chantal and Quade are close by. How long will you be gone?"

"Four or five days." His gaze flicked across at her, direct, serious. "You will be here when I get back?"

"I'm not going to leave because you kissed me, if that's what you're asking."

"Yes," he said emphatically, "that is exactly what I'm asking. I couldn't go through that again, Em. Knowing you'd run away because I lost it for a minute."

This time she didn't bother with her usual correction. She'd told him to forget the past, to let it go, and she had to do the same. To forget that, while he'd lost it for a minute, she'd lost it totally. "Don't worry about it, Mitch, really. We both lost it back there with the stress and the argument and all. It was only a kiss."

"You're really all right about that?"

Somehow she managed a reasonable smile and a little I'm-fine shrug. She even managed to meet his eyes while she out-and-out lied. "Absolutely."

When he left for Sydney two days later, Emily issued a huge sigh of relief and relaxed. She also couldn't resist reaching for a phone directory because, once she stopped thinking about that kiss—only a kiss? ha!—she remembered that she had been driving quite well before her inane reaction in the lay-by.

Yes, she would take some lessons, under her own steam. A birthday present to herself and, she hoped, a surprise for Mitch on his return. Childish, maybe, but she kept picturing herself hopping confidently behind the wheel and taking off with a cheerful wave while his mouth dropped open in shock and awe.

After scanning two columns of driving instructors, her mouth went slack. Random selection of a school did not seem the best solution—she needed some local knowledge, and who better in that field than Chantal? Of course, she poo-pooed professional lessons, insisting Emily save her money and use Quade and Julia as teachers. After all, she would need to borrow a car to get into Cliffton to the driving school.

She spent the next three days driving all over the countryside under Quade or Julia's tutelage, and finally, this afternoon, she was driving alone. A self-satisfied smile curled her lips. Of course, she hadn't yet taken on the night or the rain, although this morning she had driven in town.

Stopped at Cliffton's only traffic light, she'd felt a light-headed wave of panic, but she beat it down and poked her tongue out at it. Quade had given her a long sideways look, but she'd just smiled. She couldn't recall the last time she'd felt so good about something she'd done for herself. Remembering now, another burst of happy, satisfied pride bubbled through her blood.

Almost home from her first solo spin, the cell phone Mitch insisted she carry—"I want you and Joshua contactable at all times"—rang. As she pulled over to the side of the road, her heart jitterbugged with anticipation. But it wasn't Mitch; it was Julia, and she sounded uncharacteristically rattled.

Emily's dancing heart stalled. She'd left Joshua in Quade's care so she could practice her solo-driving without any distraction. "Is it Joshua?"

"No, nothing's wrong," Julia reassured her quickly. "I was hoping you could do me and Zane a big favor. Our baby-sitter for this evening just canceled. I know it's last minute and all, but I'm sure

Joshua can stay a bit longer with Quade and Chantal… It's only for a couple of hours.''

Julia had her at *nothing's wrong.* "I'd love to. What time?''

"Is five too early? I'll send Zane out to get you—''

"No, don't do that. I'm sure I can use Chantal's car—I've had it most of the week.'' Emily ignored the flutter of her pulse. This was her big chance to start driving after dark. With Joshua for company on the trip home, she could do it. "We'll be there at five,'' she finished decisively.

"Surprise!"

No kidding. Emily slapped a hand to her mouth as a small but rowdy bunch of well-wishers emerged from various doorways in Julia's hallway, blowing party tooters and yelling, "Happy Birthday.''

"Surprised?'' A beaming Julia immediately wrapped her in the biggest, warmest, squeeziest hug, which only caused Emily's eyes to well with happy tears.

"Does this mean I don't get to sit Bridie?'' she managed before Chantal and Quade and Zane and his sister Kree and Suzie from the Lion and a half dozen others added their own hugs and kisses.

"I *knew* the baby-sitting ruse would get you here.'' Linking arms, Julia led her through to her cozy living room with its chintz-covered chairs and rose-printed wallpaper…and balloons and streamers and a huge banner spelling Happy Birthday, Super-Em. "Next step was kidnapping because we weren't letting all these decorations go to waste.''

Joshua bounded around, beside himself with excitement. "I love birthdays," he chirped. "We got a cake with this many candles."

He held up an indeterminate number of fingers—possibly seven, although Emily's brimming eyes hampered her vision. Behind her a champagne bottle popped, and everyone cheered while she wiped her eyes with the sleeve of her ratty sweatshirt. Baby-sitting wear, not party wear.

"Why is Emmy crying?" Joshua asked, his brow puckered with concern.

"She's just surprised." Chantal thrust a glass of champagne into her hand, and Julia insisted she sit. "Right here next to me, birthday girl." And there was food—boy, was there food!—and a cake with more candles than she and Joshua combined could blow out, and someone—possibly Julia—insisted she make a wish.

A hush fell over the group, a quiet that made the thump of Emily's heart echo in her ears. What the heck was she supposed to wish for? The unimaginable, the unattainable, the unthinkable? She looked around, face-to-expectant-face and saw *his* family. Yes, they were throwing a better celebration than any her own family had conceived in her twenty-five years, but she wanted such a family for herself. Not a loaner until she moved on to her next job, but her own family, her own happiness, and while she closed her eyes and made her wish, deep down she knew it was too much to ask, too much to expect. Still, she smiled and said, "Done," and everyone cheered and sang the birthday song, and the tightness in her chest started to ease.

Later she opened her presents. A superhero bear from Joshua—"'Cuz you prol'ly miss Bruiser, since you loaned him to me''—generated more tears, not because she missed her old Bruiser bear but because of the solemn intent in his hazel eyes, so serious, like his father's.

''He's some kid,'' Chantal murmured at her side.

''I'm pretty crazy about him,'' Emily admitted as she opened the gift box from Chantal and Quade. *Along with his father and the whole extended family.* Her breath hitched in her lungs. Resting in a nest of cream tissue paper sat the most beautiful peach-colored robe ever created.

''It feels like cashmere,'' Chantal explained as Emily fingered the unbelievably soft fabric, ''but it's just a clever imitation. Doesn't it make you want to curl up and sleep with it?''

''It's exquisite,'' Emily whispered over the latest rush of tears. ''But it's too much.''

''Rubbish. Try it on,'' Chantal demanded, shooing the males from the room.

Emily did try it on, over the fancy forget-me-not-print underwear set from Julia, and as she felt the first kiss of that luxurious fabric against her bare skin she thought she might never take it off.

Kree presented her with a voucher for a cut and treatment at her hair salon, and Suzie's basket of lotions and potions brought a collective gasp from all the women. Kree clapped her hands with delight and yelled, ''Makeover,'' and no one paid any mind to Emily's objections.

''Gorgeous,'' Kree declared an hour later, admiring her handiwork as she peered into Emily's face. ''Except…''

She ducked from the room and returned wielding scissors which she clicked with scary fervor. Julia's eyes widened in—possibly mock, possibly real—horror. "Good grief, Emily, don't let her near your hair with scissors."

"Rubbish," Chantal interjected. "She's the best snipper this side of the mountains."

The sisters argued, Kree circled with a predatory gleam in her eyes, and Emily took another sip of champagne and wondered when she'd stepped through the looking glass. And then she lifted her glass to her mouth, and the plush robe moved against her skin in a sensual caress that made her forget she was plain, old, vanilla variety Emily, indispensable nanny but as attractive as a sodden kitten. Wearing designer-label underwear and an imported robe, skin shimmering with sumptuous creams, she felt like some sleek, pampered exotic.

With a particularly un-Emily-like flourish, she raised her glass toward the circling Kree in a solemn salute and invited her and her scissors to "Do your worst!"

Seven

They were home.

The twisted knot of anxiety in Mitch's gut unraveled as Korringal—with lights glowing—came into view at the end of the drive. He reached for the cell phone he'd tossed aside fifty miles back and checked for a signal. He must have called a dozen times since leaving Sydney, before he lost coverage coming over the mountains. Home phone, cell phone, Chantal's— no answer anywhere. And those last fifty miles had blurred with images of accidents, Joshua lost, Emily deciding—with him due home tomorrow—that it hadn't been "only a kiss" and that she couldn't trust living in the same house any longer.

He hit redial, impatiently tapping the wheel through three rings before—

"Hello."

Absurdly happy to hear her voice, absurdly relieved

she hadn't taken off, he said the first thing that came to mind. "You're home."

"Only just. Joshua's in bed and I'm sitting here—" She stopped abruptly. "Never mind. Where are you?"

"Pulling up outside." He enjoyed the long beat of pause as he switched off the engine. Pictured her brow puckering in a frown. "I didn't want to scare you coming in the door unannounced at this time of night."

"Outside…as in *here?*"

Mitch laughed at her astonishment. Hell, he laughed because, for the first time since that aborted driving lesson, he'd coaxed an unmeasured, knee-jerk response from Emily. He slammed the car door and took the three steps onto the verandah in one bound. "As in coming through the front door. I'll see you in a minute."

He saw her in five seconds, standing in the middle of the sitting room, the hands-free still at her ear.

"Hi," he said from the doorway, pocketing his phone. Smiling.

"Hi." She smiled back for a long, unguarded second, before she seemed to grab ahold of herself. She lowered the handset with a wry what-am-I-doing? edge to her smile. "You're a day early."

"I tried to call earlier, but…" He shrugged.

"We weren't home. Joshua is going to go bananas."

"He's asleep?"

"He's in bed," she clarified. "I'll go see if he's—"

"Wait." He crossed the room with no particular clue what he was doing, only that he didn't want her gone. He stopped in front of her. "What about you, Emily, any chance of you going bananas because I'm home?"

She laughed, a soft burst of disbelief. Then something she saw in his eyes caused her laughter to hitch, her smile to waver. And she just stood there looking at him, all uncertain cinnamon eyes and... Mitch frowned. There was something different about her. He took a step back, inspecting the entire picture.

"Your hair..."

Self-conscious, she lifted a hand to the feathery layers that framed her face. "Kree O'Sullivan cut it. I'm not quite used to the change yet."

"It looks—" grown-up, sexy, dynamite "—good."

Pleasure softened the nervous uncertainty in her eyes, even softened the edges of Mitch's need to touch her hot, new hairstyle, her skin, her mouth, the robe he'd never seen before. He cleared the heat from his throat. "Is that new, too?"

Slowly, as if his meaning took a while to sink in, she looked down. Smiled. "Yes. It's my birthday present from Chantal and Quade."

"Nice." Which didn't even begin to describe how the soft fabric skimmed her curves. Like the wicked glide of a lover's hands, not nice, not good, not professional. Mitch, the boss, forced his eyes back to her face while Mitch, the man, snarled in protest. "Happy birthday, Em."

"Thank you," she said simply.

"And has it been a happy birthday?"

"Are you kidding?" Her smile unfurled like a golden ribbon of sunshine. "Your sisters threw a party—that's where we were tonight, at Julia's—and it was a complete surprise. I had no idea.''

Nor had Mitch. And he'd talked to Chantal the previous day, to Joshua that morning. If he'd known he'd have...*what? Bought her a gift—something as hot and wicked and sexy as that robe? Fine idea, boss.* Shucking aside a ridiculous sense of disappointment, he focused on the unlikely event of his family keeping closemouthed about anything. ''A surprise party, huh? And no one let the cat out of the bag?''

''I suspect it was last minute. Julia rang in an apparent flap to ask me to baby-sit—she is an excellent actress, by the way—and they were all there when I arrived. There were decorations and a cake and—'' She stopped, shamefaced, and winced. ''I'm rambling. Sorry. Can I blame it on the champagne? Sugar overload from the cake?''

''Sure you can,'' he said softly. As for the ebullience racing through his blood at the same breakneck speed—he blamed scented skin and a peach-skin robe, the gleam of excitement in her eyes and the pink flush of delight on her face. He blamed a week without her company and a year without any woman's and the last hour hammering home, not knowing if she were here or gone. ''Was it Julia's special cake?'' he asked. ''The fluffy chocolate one with all the layers?''

''Yes! With raspberries on top and totally slathered in whipped cream!''

Now there was an image he didn't need right now. The birthday girl with her hot new hairstyle, opening the wraparound robe and saying something such as—

''Would you like some?''

—in her shyly sexy voice. Mitch might have

groaned out loud, although he did try to contain the hot, hungry sound.

"We brought the leftovers home," she finished, her voice trailing off uncertainly. Maybe he hadn't groaned, but she definitely sensed the shift in mood. She swallowed, lifted a hand to touch her throat. The small, nervous gesture resonated through Mitch's body like an erotic whisper.

Tempt me, touch me, taste me.

A step closer and her nostrils flared slightly, scenting him, his purpose. Her lashes fluttered over darkened eyes, and he reached out as slow as the night to stroke the warm, smooth skin of her throat. Satin. Baby soft. He traced the fading scar of the scratch incurred that night in the forest, and his gut stirred with more than the raw, unruly surge of lust. Something rich and tender and multifaceted that jolted him back into his own space.

"I..." Emily forced in air, forced her throat and her voice and her brain to start working again. She waved a vague hand toward the kitchen. "I'll just go get you that—"

"Daddy!" A four-year-old dervish tore through the doorway and threw himself at his father. Whatever she'd been about to fetch quit Emily's mind, knocked out of the park by the scene before her. One of Mitch's broad hands cupped his son's fair head; Joshua's sturdy arms circled his father's neck. Bowled over, like Emily, by Mitch's unexpected appearance, he didn't say a word for at least twenty seconds, but then the questions erupted, a volatile stream of whys and hows and didyas with no space for answers. Mitch laughed, a deep, rusty sound

packed full of tenderness, and told him to put a brake on it.

Emily started to back away, wishing she could put a brake on her emotions. *This* was her birthday wish. To be down there on the floor, part of that embrace, belonging. Loved. She started to back away but she couldn't look away, couldn't tear herself away.

"Didya bring me anything?" Joshua asked for at least the third time.

"A hug?"

Clearly delighted, he giggled. "What about Emmy? Didya get her a hug, too?"

Emily's breath caught in her throat as Mitch looked up, right into her eyes. A memory of that earlier heat flared between them, quick, deep, insidious. Then he smiled and said, "No. Better."

Better than belonging in that embrace? Impossible.

"What, Daddy, what?" Joshua captured his father's face between his hands, forcing his attention away from Emily, which was perfectly fine by her. She needed to start breathing again, to school her face and her responses, to remember she was only the nanny.

"A car," Mitch said casually, and her heart stalled.

"Is it a sports car? A red one like Chantal's?"

"If it was a sports car like Chantal's—" with quick hands, Mitch flipped Joshua onto his shoulders "—how would we get the skis on top?"

A car *with skis on top?* Was he teasing? She opened her mouth to ask but he was already striding for the door, Joshua calling back to her in excitement. "Come on, Emmy. Come see your new car. It's got skis."

* * *

Three sets of skis, she counted from her vantage point on the verandah. Her heart plummeted faster than an out-of-control ski lift…which happened to be approximately the same speed she had plummeted down the mountain the last time someone had strapped planks of timber to her feet. Head over ski over tail.

But right after that initial response came a second thought. Annabelle's parents ran a ski lodge. That's how Emily had come to take that tumble, the one winter holiday she'd taken with the family. Did this mean Mitch had changed his mind, taken her advice, contacted the Blaineys?

Eyes wide, she swung around to ask, but was immediately distracted by his grin as he lowered his frenetically excited son to the ground. "So, what do you think?"

"Are you going to Corrong?"

His grin dimmed. "Yes, but not because of Randall and Janet, if that's what you're thinking. A group from TVTWO had a weekend planned, and they suggested I join them—there are some ideas floating around for a second series."

"But you will contact them? I mean, if you're going to be right there in the same village?"

Before he could answer, Joshua finished his first lap of the new vehicle and stopped, his brow puckered. "Where's your truck, Daddy?"

"I had to leave it in Sydney, at the apartment. I'll pick it up next time we're in town." He switched his attention to Emily. "You haven't said what you think of the car?"

The car. Right. That would be the thing *wearing* the skis. She took her first good look at the compact

SUV, silver, sporty and brand-spanking-new. She frowned. "It looks…expensive. I don't think—"

"It's safe," Mitch cut in. "For Joshua and for you."

"D'you like it, Em?" Joshua asked earnestly. He kicked a tire. "It looks like it goes fast."

How could she not smile? And how could she object to the safety argument? It wasn't her car, really, it was Joshua's. As his nanny, she got to drive it, that's all.

"How's the driving going?" Mitch asked. Via his regular phone calls from Sydney, she'd kept him informed, albeit in a cautious manner. He hadn't said a word about her making her own plans for the lessons, about not waiting for his return.

"Coming along," she answered now, cautious as ever.

"Emmy drove on her own," Joshua supplied. "It was her first time."

"I'm sorry I missed that."

At that quiet admission—or perhaps the flash of intensity in his expression—her heart did a crazy little two-step. "This afternoon. And I drove into Julia's, before the party."

One brow arched. "I'm impressed."

"Don't be," she said quickly. "I'm pretty sure I would have wimped out on the driving-home-in-the-dark leg, even if there'd been no champagne as an excuse."

"Quade drove us home. His car's got six gears. How many does Emmy's have?"

While Mitch rattled off a list of features that made her head spin and opened a door so Joshua could check it all out for himself, Emily absently rubbed her hands up her arms, back down again, recalling the heady wave of relief when Quade said she couldn't drive home. She was such a coward.

"Cold?" Mitch asked, back at her side.

She shook her head. She was never cold with him standing so close, telling her things like, "You did great, Em, driving on your own," and looking for all the world as if he meant it. She ached to thank him for those words, to wrap her arms around *him*, to simply be held. But she was such a coward.

"Hey!" Joshua yelled. "Is this for *me?* It must be for me 'cuz Emmy's already got a hun'red bears."

An embarrassed flush warmed her face. "Not quite that many."

Joshua clambered down from the vehicle, clutching a fierce-faced brown bear. "You want to go introduce him to Bruiser?" Mitch suggested. "His name's Halt."

Emily followed Joshua into the house. "Strange name."

"Halt, Who Goes Bear," Mitch explained, closing the door behind them. "I thought he might be a useful addition to sentry duties at night."

"Nice thought," Emily said softly. He grinned, and her heart turned over.

"I have my moments."

Oh, yes, indeed he did.

How could she not be crazy about a man who chose such a perfect gift for his son?

Crazy. Emily shook her head. That was the only word to describe her state of mind following Mitch's return, because half an hour later she had agreed to go skiing, even though she classified her only experience on the slopes as a disaster, grade A. But, humming with the warm and fuzzy remnants of the father-son-bear episode and her birthday party and her modest driving success, she would likely have said, "Sure, Mitch," if he'd asked her to go jump off the top of Mount Tibaroo.

Instead he'd asked her along on the ski weekend, and she'd said, "Sure, Mitch," because even though the lodge where he'd booked an apartment provided a Ski Kids program, he needed her to look after Joshua while he schmoozed with the TV crowd. So, here she stood in her borrowed clothes—Chantal to the rescue!—juggling skis and poles and gloves because Mitch insisted she try skiing one more time. And because when he smiled at her a certain way, she forgot to think and made crazy choices.

"Can I help you?"

"Probably not," Emily told the young ski instructor. "But I'm here to give it a go."

"You haven't skied before, huh?"

"Not successfully," Emily admitted.

"Well, that's about to change. I'll have you gliding down this mountain before you can say ski bunny."

Mitch enjoyed his first hour on the mountain. He'd have enjoyed it more but for a nagging sense of unease. Not due to Joshua—he was carving up the slopes in the Ski Kids squad. He knew because he'd checked.

As for Emily…

He shouldn't have left her. Sure, she'd chosen a lesson at the ski school, preferring to fall on her butt without him watching, thank you very much. Sure, she'd pasted a carefree smile on her face as she waved him off from the lesson area. But just before he took the first bend, he'd looked back, and that last visual had burned itself into the back of his brain.

One small figure in a red jacket, standing all alone.

Halfway up the long haul from Demon Gully on a stalled lift, he checked his watch again. Cursed again. Fifteen minutes since her lesson finished and he'd aimed to be there. Just to check she was all right. Fifteen bloody minutes on a stalled chairlift.

With a grinding lurch the lift started, stopped, started again. A mocking cheer rolled through the passenger load. "About time," his neighbor muttered.

Yeah. Mitch smiled politely, felt the tension in his facial muscles and grimaced. What was with him? Letting this vague, unfounded concern for Emily sour what should have been a perfect morning. Hell, she was probably relaxing in a café by now, enjoying time to herself, sipping her hot chocolate, a satisfied smile softening her lips because she'd slayed the first lesson. Because she'd had a ball flirting with Fritz or Alberto or whichever-the-hell-ski-instructor had helped her up when she'd fallen on her butt.

Thinking about Emily's butt didn't relax him a whole lot. Skiing off the lift and seeing her did. Despite the crowd and the distance, he picked her out immediately, red jacket vivid against the blinding whiteness, her platinum hair equally dramatic against her jacket. As he watched her tramp along the trail leading to their lodge, relief whistled from his lungs. Obviously, she was fine. Obviously, she'd had enough for her first day and was heading home.

Obviously, he needed to make sure.

On skis he quickly cut down the distance between them, weaving in and out of traffic until he caught up just shy of the lodge. Slogging it out, skis on shoulder, head down, she didn't see him until he swooshed to a stop in her path. Her head came up, her shoulders straightened.

"Hey." Mitch smiled down at her, warmth washing through him, until he realized she looked more than surprised by his sudden appearance. She looked…shaken.

"Hey, yourself."

Despite the glib reply, her smile was as wan as her face, as pale as the snow in her hair, on her jacket, her pants. He brushed a clump from her sleeve. "You been rolling in this stuff?"

"Not intentionally." Her shoulders slumped forward again. "It just kind of happened every time I tried to get up."

"Fritz wasn't there to help you?"

A small frown drew her brows together. "Fritz?"

"Private joke." Private and hardly a joke, since it made him steam instead of laugh. He clicked out of his skis, relieved her of hers and jammed the lot into a thick snowdrift beside their lodge.

"Shouldn't they go in the racks?" she asked.

"They'll be fine here until we go out again."

She held up a hand, gloved and not quite steady, and shuddered. Actually shuddered. "Speak for yourself."

"You didn't enjoy your lesson?"

"Skiing is way overrated. Not to mention dangerous."

Everything inside him stilled. "Dangerous, *how?* Did you hurt yourself?"

"It was nothing—"

"Hell, you're shaking like a leaf. That's not nothing."

"I have snow in my pants, I'm cold." She started tugging at her gloves and when one refused to budge, she swore. So un-Emily-like. "You know I *was* having fun. I fell over a few times but by the end of the lesson I was starting to get it. And I decided to do one more run, on my own, and I took a wrong turn and it was steep and I...I..."

"It's okay, Em—"

"It's not okay!" Her voice shook. Her hands shook. And he could see she was perilously close to tears. "I can't even get these rotten gloves off!"

"Here, let me."

Being Emily, she tried to stop him—she'd been looking out for herself for so long, she didn't expect help—but Mitch brushed her objections aside. Then he picked her up and carried her to the lodge. She clung to him awkwardly as he clumped up the metal steps, murmuring something about being too heavy.

"You? Heavy?" To prove his point, he tossed her a little, caught her closer to his body. He enjoyed the gasp of surprise, the way color returned to her cheeks and the fit of her curves against him.

That he enjoyed a little too much.

At the locked door she started to squirm, wanting down, a perfectly sensible thing to want. *Remember the last time she wiggled in your arms. Remember how that ended. Is that what you want? Kissing, angst, passion unresolved.*

"Where's the key?" she asked, her breath warm against the side of his neck. *Put her down, get out the key, open the door.*

"Inside jacket pocket, right-hand side." He stared

straight ahead at the door, listening to the echo of his voice, low, gruff, turned on. Ignoring the voice of logic in his head.

"I'll have to undo your zip."

"That would definitely make it easier."

Upper body twisting, she angled herself to gain purchase on his zipper, and he felt the soft pressure of one breast against his chest—momentary, momentous—before she shifted again. Then he heard his breath catch, his pulse hike, and the soft rasp of his jacket opening. Heat hummed in his blood and his ears as her small, soft hand reached inside. *It's only your jacket, for cripe's sake, not your pants. Get a grip.*

"Got it," she declared much too quickly, twisting the other way, bumping her rounded backside against his body, dragging the smooth line of her thigh against that part of him that craved contact.

Mitch sucked in a hot breath, rocked back on his heels, and her eyes widened. Knowingly. For a moment he let the knowledge of his arousal wrap them in heat, a binding fire of want acknowledged. Then he expelled the air on a fragmented sigh. "I'm guessing I should reassess my plan to get you inside and out of those wet clothes."

He tried for light, a quip to take an edge off the stifling tension, but she didn't smile. Her mouth opened, closed—yeah, she had a right to be speechless—and her dark eyes churned with uneasy, misty heat. He put her down, right there beside the door, but he couldn't for the life of him move away. Despite that uneasiness in her eyes. He unpopped the top two buttons of her jacket, started unwinding the scarf from her neck.

"I'm guessing," she began, her voice husky edged, "you think I'm incapable of getting out of them by myself."

"You were experiencing some trouble with the gloves."

"Yeah." She blew out a breath, hot, exasperated. "I was half-frozen and spitting mad with myself."

"Because you fell? You did fine. You need more practice is all." He touched the side of her face, was surprised to find it cool. Unlike her eyes or her voice.

"Please don't patronize me," she blazed. "I did not 'do fine' and that seems to have become a feature of my life lately."

Mitch frowned. "What about your driving?"

"I drove in the daytime, on country roads. Give me night in the rain in the city and let's see how fine I do." She huffed out another breath. "I couldn't even keep a job cleaning hotel rooms, for pity's sake. I ended up taking charity accommodation from your sister and a job with you—"

"Is that so bad?" he asked.

"Yes. No." She laughed, a low, rough sound full of self-derision. But then she looked up at him, all big, troubled eyes, and his chest tightened with an almost painful depth of emotion. "I hate feeling like a victim, Mitch. I want to feel strong, I want to have choices. I want to be able to…do stuff."

"From where I'm standing you're not doing so bad on the important 'stuff.'" When she opened her mouth to protest, that tight ache in his chest flared with impatience. "You cared for your sick grandfather when no one else gave a damn, you know how to soothe a child's night fears and build his esteem. You turn a household routine from a shambles into a smoothly oiled machine, and you're upset because you can't ski?"

"Not upset," she returned, as if she'd missed everything that went before. "Weak. Mad. Frustrated."

You and me both. He shook his head, far from understanding. "You want to ski? Fine, we'll ski."

Her gaze leaped to his, wide and edgy. *"Now?"*

"Do you want to learn to do this or not?"

Although she straightened her shoulders and nodded, she didn't look at all certain. "Yes, but Joshua finishes Ski Kids in an hour. And aren't you supposed to be meeting up with the TV crew for lunch? Isn't that the reason we're here?"

She was right, on all counts, but he wasn't letting this go. "Tomorrow morning, then." He hunkered down and looked into her face. "I'll get you skiing, Em."

"Funny, but my instructor said the self-same thing."

"No doubt," he said shortly. "But I mean it."

Eight

Heart thumping wildly, Emily studied the ski run before them, a ski run that appeared to plunge away from the summit like a roller-coaster descent.

"Are you sure you have time for this?" she asked the man at her side, hating the desperate edge to her voice. Hating that her painful confession the previous day had led to this current predicament. "I mean, I did pretty well on the bunny slope and I'm happy with—"

"You wanted to ski," Mitch interrupted mildly. "So quit trying to get out of this."

Emily made one last attempt to deflect his attention. "You could be spending this time with the Blaineys, you know."

"I'm spending time with them later."

Emily's eyes widened. "You *did* call them? Why didn't you tell me? When are you meeting them?"

"I left a message, said I'd call at their lodge at twelve," he said cautiously. "It's just a meeting."

"I'm glad you made the first move." So very, very glad for Joshua's sake and for Mitch's sake. He needed to make this peace.

"Yeah, well, if it doesn't go so well I have the perfect antidote lined up." An unholy light gleamed in the depths of his eyes. "We're skiing Devil's Revenge."

She didn't know anything about that ski run, but its demonic name conjured images of a near-vertical drop with jagged rocks and bodies plunging out of control. A cold thread of fear wound through her "We…who?"

He laughed—he actually laughed out loud—at r squeaky, terror-filled question. "Not you, sweeth t. A few of the guys."

And something in his eyes, in that laugh and the way he said "guys," raised Emily's hackles in a completely different way to her previous fear. "Is this one of those macho, chest-thumping, male-bonding things?"

Dressed broad shoulders to boots in black ski attire, *he* looked like one of those macho, chest-thumping males. He was also grinning. "You could call it that."

"Or you could call it insane." Another image of that demonic run flashed through her mind, and anxiety turned her expression serious. "Isn't it dangerous?"

"Only if you take risks," he said evenly. He stabbed both his poles into the snow. "And I don't."

Trepidation churned in Emily's belly as he glided to a stop in front of her.

"Time to get you skiing," he said smoothly. "Hand over your poles."

Emily blinked. He wanted her to relinquish her support system? Her only reliable connection with mother earth? She ran her tongue around a powder-dry mouth. "You can't be serious."

He didn't laugh. In fact, when he leaned forward and whipped the ski-goggles from her face, his eyes glinted with purpose. "You won't be needing those, either."

"I won't?"

"You won't." He smiled, probably for reassurance, although Emily remained thoroughly unreassured. Her heart thudded against her rib cage as if begging for escape. It had her sympathy.

"Before we came up here, you said this run—" she sneaked an aggrieved look around him at the roller-coaster mountain "—you said it wasn't much steeper than the bunny slope."

"And before we started this morning, you said you trusted me. Remember?"

Would she ever forget? Hands on her shoulders, he'd leaned right in close and captured her gaze, her focus, her entire being. Then, in that low, husky, velvet-cream voice, he'd asked for her trust. Heavens, if he'd asked for her right arm with that kind of in-her-face sincerity, she'd have gladly chopped it off.

Perhaps she should have offered that alternative: Here, Mitch, take my arm instead. I'd as soon hang on to my trust, if it's all the same with you.

Except she did trust him and always had.

Eyes squeezed shut, she drew a deep, sustaining breath and uncurled her gloved hands from the poles. "Take them. Quickly, before I change my mind."

His laugh was low and engaging and so close she felt it fan her face, a deliciously warm contrast to the cold mountain air. Her eyes snapped open, and he smiled right into them. "Good girl. That's all you have to do," he said softly, slowly. "Keep looking right into my eyes."

Oh, yeah. She could manage that. Without any effort.

Belly tight and knees weak, she did as he asked. Dimly she noticed that he'd taken her hands and wrapped them around the center of her ski poles before positioning his on either side. Warmth spun through her body, eddying out from that hand-beside-hand contact but mostly from the prolonged eye contact.

Ah, those eyes… Reassuring, yes; purposeful, yes; but something else lurked deeper, swirling in the ever-changing mix of green and gray. Then he started to move. No, *they* started to move. Skiing backward, he towed her by the poles they both held, her skis sliding inside his but unstable, wobbly, as feeble as her knees. She squeaked a warning.

Unperturbed he raised one brow. "Where's your weight, Emily?"

Um…drowning in your eyes?

"Balls of your feet, skis parallel," he instructed. "No, don't look down—"

"How will I know if my skis are straight?"

"Were you looking at them earlier?"

She frowned. The bunny slope where they'd started had teemed with learners, most as inept as she. "I had to watch out I didn't run anyone down."

"And you managed to keep your skis straight? Without looking down?"

Mostly. With a small nod she acknowledged his point and relaxed a smidgen. They traversed the wide basin in a big, lazy serpentine crawl, gathering speed gradually and turning on the thickly powdered banks. Not that she didn't blunder. Several times she managed to cross her tips, and her stomach jittered in instant panic. But his calm purpose steadied her, reassured her, fed her confidence.

When they detoured off the main thoroughfare— "Gets icy lower down," he explained—onto a trail that weaved its way between the tall, straight snow gums, Emily's heart bumped along with their skis.

"It's okay," he murmured. "I've got you."

Oh, yes, he had her. Especially when he took one of her hands from the poles and held it in his strong grip.

"Let go the other one," he encouraged. "It's time to start trusting yourself. You can do it, Emily. Believe it."

Letting go wasn't so difficult—her fingers, surprisingly, hadn't frozen into a death grip. He held her hand a minute longer, and then his fingers slipped away and her heart dipped momentarily with the loss, before skipping into a faster rhythm. Without the tow poles, without a guiding hand, her skis continued to glide smoothly inside his, following his lead in a fluid, graceful dance.

"Do you *feel* your skis running?" he asked.

Amazingly, she did. Even more amazingly, she remembered to shift her weight, ski to ski, as he led her through a sharp turn. Approval darkened his eyes, and her heart smiled with silent joy. *Yes,* it beamed. *You've got it.* For the first time in her life she felt

athletic, accomplished, almost daredevilish, and her
grin spread all over her face.

"Having fun yet?" he asked.

"Are you kidding? I feel like thumping *my* chest."

Mitch laughed, and the sound seemed to soar as
big and bright as the perfect winter sky. Even more
exhilarating than the crisp swoosh of skis against
snow, she mused, was the sound of his laughter.

"You are a good teacher," she admitted as they
executed another tricky turn. "Chantal was wrong."

"Don't tell *her* that." Their eyes met and shared
the humor a moment, before his expression turned
serious. "I didn't do so well at the driving instruc-
tion."

"That wasn't your fault."

"No?"

"No." Was it her imagination or did his gaze dip
to her mouth? Her smile faltered; her lips tingled with
heat. No, not her imagination. Undercurrents of that
day, of how it ended, swirled around them, binding
them as firmly as their synchronized motion.

"I shouldn't have kissed you," he said quietly, and
the sound of that word—that slow, sibilant *kiss*
word—shimmered through her as delectably as the
first touch of his lips.

"Why not?"

"I'm your employer."

"Not twenty-four hours a day and not on Sundays.
Besides—" Their skis touched and bumped.

"Easy," he murmured, slowing their speed, bal-
ancing her with his firm hands on her upper arms,
drawing her so close that their knees brushed in a
sensual slide. "Besides?" he prompted.

"I wanted you to kiss me."

Not a good time to shock him, Emily decided, when he stopped without warning. Her skis continued, delivering her right into his solid body with a *whoomph*. If her skis hadn't kept on sliding she might not have wrapped her arms around him, but her skis *did* keep sliding and for this she said a silent, Thank you, Monsieur Rossignol.

Before letting go she savored the moment, committing the details to memory. The hard strength of his body flush with hers, the mingled scents of fresh air and sandalwood and warm man. His hands sliding over her back in a way that felt deliciously like a caress, his long exhalation against her hair.

A low laugh that mirrored the tension in his body.

Gently he eased her away, enough to look down into her eyes. "You shouldn't go saying things like that."

Perhaps it *was* time to say things like that. Last week she'd driven a car. Just now she'd skied. Perhaps it was time to go after something that really mattered—the reality instead of the symbol. Her hand trembled as she lifted it to touch his mouth...and she wished her thick gloves to perdition.

Slowly she traced the curve of his bottom lip. "I wanted you to kiss me yesterday, too. When you carried me up those stairs."

"And now?"

"It's Sunday." You're not my boss, I'm not your nanny, so please kiss me before I expire with need.

Desire glittered in his eyes, sharp, intense. Emily trembled as he took her face in his gloved hands, big hands that framed her entire jaw and cheeks. And then he bent and took her lips with the same firm, all-encompassing purpose. Emily's entire tense, strung-out body sighed with relief.

Six months before, he'd kissed her in anguish, a sightless, senseless quest for comfort, for life in the nearest shape and form. That day in the rain he'd kissed her in frustration but this…*this* was a real kiss. A real toe-curling, knee-weakening, thigh-softening kiss that started with the lips but slid through her blood in quicksilver flashes of heat.

He tasted her lips all at once, then in tiny nibbling samples, before drawing her bottom lip between his teeth in a gentle sense-shivering bite. Who knew that kissing could be such an art, such a skill, so involved and involving? And then—she dragged a serrated breath into her aching lungs—and then he led her tongue in an unhurried duel of astonishing eroticism, a give-and-take dance that mimicked the way they'd slid over the snow. Mouth to mouth, she followed his lead, learning and exploring, fanning the slow fire in her blood.

Oh, yes, Chantal had been so wrong about his teaching skills. So very, very wrong.

Hands at his nape, fingers tunneling into his hair, she pressed closer, restlessly seeking that perfect alignment of soft against hard. Up. She needed to push up on her toes, to wind her leg around his.

Too late she recognized the impediment. The tip of her ski lodged in the snow, twisting her knee, throwing them both off balance until they collapsed in a tangle of skis and limbs. For one stunned second all she heard was rough, fractured breathing—hers? his?—and then a voice, a stranger's voice raised to attract attention, cut across the slopes. "Are you all right over there?"

Emily blinked snow from her eyelashes, brushed it from her face. Had she landed nose first? *Was* she all right? The planks attached to her feet complicated all attempts to right herself. Her attempts to right herself brought her deliciously, thrillingly closer to the man who had broken her fall. Amazing that planes so hard could provide such perfect cushioning.

"*Are* you all right?" he asked.

Oh, yes, she decided. I'm about drowning in all-rightness. She wiggled some more for the sheer thrill of moving against his body, heard his swift intake of breath, felt strong hands close over her hips and the thick pounding of her own pulse. But then those hands set her aside and he busied himself with binding releases, freeing her with a couple of quick, efficient clicks. Emily flopped back in the snow, eyes squinted against the dazzling brightness until a shadow blocked out the sun.

"Do you need a hand?" The passerby who'd called out had come to their rescue.

"No," Mitch growled. "I have two of my own."

Mr. Helpful backed away. Quickly, if the crisp crack of skis on snow was anything to go by. "Thanks for stopping," Emily called after him. He didn't answer.

The ensuing silence resonated with the tension of Mitch's curt response. It snapped around them, as edgy as the sound of those departing skis. She wondered if their good Samaritan had put two and two together and come up with two-idiots-trying-to-make-out-on-skis. She'd been lying in the snow thinking in terms of shedding clothes, for pity's sake. Unexpected and unbidden, laughter bubbled up inside her, part tension, part genuine amusement, and once she started she couldn't seem to stop.

"What's so funny?"

Unable to form a meaningful answer, she shook her head, enough times that the snow pillow beneath registered as cold and wet. Not uncomfortable, but a sobering contrast to her overheated body.

"Do you think," she asked eventually, sneaking a sideways look at Mitch, "that man had any idea why we were flailing about in the snow?"

His response fell somewhere between a snort and a laugh. "After I bit his head off? Probably."

Oh, dear. Emily chewed her lip and sneaked in another quick glance. Flat on his back, he stared up into the sky, either unable or unwilling to look at her. "I suppose we should get going," she said softly, her mood sobering.

"Not yet. I need to lie here and cool off a minute longer."

Oh. His meaning slammed into her, sending her spirits soaring. Sending her gaze soaring down his body. *Oh.* She swallowed. "Perhaps you need to lie facedown," she suggested.

He groaned. Rolled onto his side. Pinned her to the spot with the intense heat of his gaze. "Perhaps you need to remember where we are."

Shocked by her own boldness—where had that last comment come from?—and his response, Emily could only stare back. Heat thrummed through her body, a dramatic counterpoint to the cold blanket of snow beneath. If they were somewhere else, somewhere warmer and drier and less exposed, would he bother trying to cool down? Or would he do something with that impressive delineation of hard heat?

A feverish shiver raced through her blood at the thought of shedding clothes, of touching, taking…

In a sudden rush of motion, he rose to his feet. Bindings clicked, one, two. "Let's go."

Shaking free of her sultry imaginings, Emily eyed his proffered hand. "That was a quick minute."

"Lying there next to you—" he expelled a harsh breath "—I was never going to cool off."

Thirty minutes waiting for the Blaineys to show— or not show—didn't cool Mitch down any. Finally, sick of waiting in the lobby while one of the staff went "to see if I can find them," he stomped back out the door. He could do without that kind of aggravation. He'd done his part, he'd made an attempt, and the frustration of a wait that had seemed more like thirty hours than minutes boiled in his blood as he made his way back to his lodge.

That cross-country slog managed to work off some steam but not nearly enough to stanch his response when he spotted Emily's racked skis. Hot, fierce impatience surged through his blood, a desire to barrel through that door, to stride through the foyer, to find her, to…*what?*

To see her eyes widen with surprise because he was back so early? To see them burn with sweet fire as she recognized his intent, as he shed clothes and conscience and control and finished what they'd started on that mountain trail?

He blew out a long, frustrated breath and let himself inside in the civilized way. Key and doorknob weren't nearly as satisfying as the notion of shoulder and brute force, and the edgy need to break something, anything, rode him hard as he flung gloves and boots and jacket aside. The thud of the door closing behind him sounded unnaturally loud and he recognized, belatedly, the concentrated quiet within the apartment.

Hands on hips, he inspected the living area. No used mug or glass on the kitchen bench. No magazine or television remote cast aside on the coffee table. He prowled through the emptiness, pausing outside her bedroom.

He knocked on her door. "Emily?"

No answer.

Damn. The punch of disappointment hit low and hard. Its power should have triggered a million alarm bells, but, hell, if he'd been listening to internal warning systems he'd not have come within a metric mile of Emily and this apartment, not with Joshua at Ski Kids for hours yet. Not with the taste of her kiss still sizzling through his blood.

Not remembering the afterward, the way her dark gaze had stroked his aroused body as he'd struggled for control. No wariness, no reservation, just pure, sweet want.

Mitch flung back his head and growled. Not a good idea, remembering, reliving. A cool-down shower might help…or he could take her advice and bury himself, facedown, in the cold, white snow. For about a week, he decided with a rueful grimace.

En route to his bedroom, he stripped off his shirt and balled it for the obligatory three-point attempt on the laundry basket. He didn't let the shot go. Alerted by a faint sound beyond the bathroom door, he paused. Felt a subtle skip in his pulse. A not-so-subtle tightening low in his body.

Slowly he lifted a hand to knock at the same time

the door slid open. Eyes wide with alarm, Emily slapped a hand to her chest and backed away from the door, back into a fragrant cloud of steam that drifted around her in delicate, ethereal ribbons. Not naked but near enough. Her birthday robe—soft, pale, peachy pink—clung to every slope and curve of her newly bathed body.

Clung and clung and clung.

Blood roared through his veins, hot, demanding, deafening any polite avert-your-eyes, give-her-some-privacy pretences. To hell with politeness. He could spend another hour staring, stripping away that robe in his imagination.

The gurgle of emptying bathwater dragged him back to reality. He inhaled, slow and deep, filling his lungs with scented steam. Raspberries and cream. Ever since the night of her birthday, he'd fantasized about those tastes on her skin. On his tongue. Riveted, he watched *her* tongue moisten her plump bottom lip.

"I didn't think you'd be back so soon."

"Nor did I," he said tightly. "My in-laws didn't show."

"Didn't show?" Her voice rose on a note of mild pique. "Why ever not?"

Annoyed, frustrated, Mitch hitched an impatient shoulder. "Your guess is as good as mine. No message, no explanation, nothing."

Questions crowded the sympathetic warmth in Emily's dark eyes. In his current mood, Mitch needed neither. Not unless the sympathy was for the ache low in his body and the questions started with, Do you want to…? and contained the words *hard, fast* and *now*.

Yeah, right, and this is Emily, for cripe's sake.

What he needed was a shower. Cold, slow and now. "I'll use the other shower—"

"I'm finished. You can have this one." Her gaze drifted to his bare chest, touched it with fingertips of flame before returning to his face. "I can recommend a bath for the kinks."

"What kinks?"

"Skiing ones, falling ones. Although I guess you don't fall down as much as I do."

Their eyes met and held, and shared recollections of falling and kissing and wanting arced between them. Color crept into her cheeks and when she drew a breath, her breasts pressed tight against her robe, tight and obviously aroused.

"I'll leave you to it." She gestured vaguely toward the shower stall. "To your shower or bath. Or whatever."

Or whatever. Right. He needed to forget about raspberries and cream on her lush body. He needed to get out of the doorway, give her some room to move, because she sure as hell was having trouble edging between the vanity and—

Her swift, sharp inhalation had him in the room and in her face in a split second. "What's wrong?"

A hint of pain darkened her eyes as she rubbed a hand up and down her thigh. "I bumped the edge of the vanity. Right on my bruise."

"What bruise?"

She sighed. "Where I fell over yesterday. It's nothing."

The unconvincing claim reverberated through Mitch, reminding him how she'd used the exact same word to describe whatever happened between them that dark, desolate night last year.

Not nothing.

As he reached down and swung her into his arms, as he absorbed her light weight and her soft "Oh" of surprise, something rich and dangerous stirred deep inside, something that froze him momentarily.

"Honestly, Mitch, it is a big, fat nothing."

There it was again. *Nothing.* The word he no longer trusted on her lips. *His* tightened with renewed purpose. "Let me be the judge of that."

Nine

Let me be the judge of that.

Emily knew she shouldn't accept such highhand-
edness, knew she should rebel against his habit of
picking her up and the lord-and-masterful way he
shouldered open the bedroom door. But how could
she summon any indignation when her insides quaked
with expectation and apprehension and pure, unadul-
terated hunger?

Because it was *his* bedroom door.

Surreptitiously she snuggled a mite closer and his
"stop wriggling" growl rumbled through his chest
right by her ear. Oh, sweet heaven. She couldn't control the response that quivered through her body. For
one breathless second his arms tightened around her
waist and thighs, curling her even closer to the hard
wall of his chest—bliss!—and then he dumped her

onto the bed so quickly her head spun. So much for expectation.

She propped herself on her elbows and eyed him narrowly. "Are you going to start chest thumping now?"

He laughed shortly. Humorlessly. "Maybe. But first I want to check these bruises of yours."

"I said it's noth—"

"Prove it."

Hot tension pulsed off him in palpable waves as he stared her down. Hot tension and something deeper, stronger, fiercer—a challenge that fed Emily's heart with courage. Her pulse thudded to the same beat as the words *prove it, prove it, prove it,* as she rolled onto one side and bared her leg, all the way to the top of her thigh.

"Satisfied?"

A muscle jumped in his jaw. An answer flamed in his eyes. *Not nearly.* And then his gaze shifted, trailing down her body to the exposed patch of black and blue. Not pretty, she knew, an opinion Mitch shared if his wince meant anything. "You bruise easily?"

"About as easily as a ripe peach." With a shaky smile and a shaking hand she flipped the robe back into place and sat up. *Stupid, stupid, stupid.* She should not have taken up that prove-it taunt. She should not have been so eager to expose her ugly mottled skin.

"Is that all?"

The curt question snapped her attention back to his face. Hooded eyes, tight lips, guarded expression. Emily frowned. "What do you mean?"

"No more damaged fruit you're hiding?"

He almost sounded like…almost looked like… *No.*

Emily got real. "Will you believe me, however I answer?"

"No."

Exactly as she'd suspected. "I guess that's the journalist in you."

"A journalist needs to know."

Simple words, softly spoken, but a multilayered message burned in his eyes as he sat down on the bed. When his bare biceps brushed Emily's shoulder, her heartbeat tripped as wildly as her thoughts. Did he mean to do more than expose her bruises?

"Sometimes a journalist has to—" with firm hands he turned her to face him and reached for the knotted tie at her waist "—uncover the truth for himself."

Mitch felt her tremble…or maybe that was him. His world definitely rocked on its axis as he peeled back the robe, as he slowly revealed her body in all its naked, voluptuous, raspberries-and-cream glory. He had never imagined, never in his wildest, hottest dreams.

Holy hell.

Dry-mouthed, speechless, he trailed his fingertips from the base of her throat to the dip of her navel. Saw her lips part, innocently wanton. Felt his body harden. How could he have seen her like this and not remember? Frustration tangled with desire in a fierce, snarled web of intensity. "I need to remember, Emily. Everything we did that night."

Denial sparked in her eyes, a denial Mitch refused to hear. He took the contradiction unspoken from her lips in a long, hard kiss, a meeting of mouths and tongues and raw passion. He knew the taste of her kiss, the stroke of her hands at his nape, but why didn't he know this body, this heat, this huge, gaping chasm of hunger?

And then her hands shifted, sliding over his shoulders to touch his bare chest with soft, shy uncertainty, and that touch, finally, stirred the black hole in his memory. Relinquishing her mouth, he grabbed her hands and held them against his skin, against the crazy lurch of his heart. "You touched me. Exactly like that."

Pink stained her cheeks; a flame of admission flickered in her eyes.

"How else, Emily?" He moved her trapped hands against him in a slow, sultry slide. "Where else?"

She shook her head, remained mutinously silent, and Mitch barely suppressed a growl. He let go of her hands but not his resolve. He would find out; he would know. A glimmer of memory wasn't nearly enough—he wanted reality, those full breasts warm and heavy in his hands, those soft, silken fingers on his body, cupping him, stroking him.

Hands on her shoulders, he eased her body down onto the mattress and the sight of her there—the sensual spread of her body framed by the shucked-back robe—was unspeakably erotic. Rays of sunlight slanted through the window and painted her hair and skin in pale, winter light—a dramatic contrast to the wine-red bedclothes and the fire-red heat in his blood.

"Did I touch you that night?" Deliberately he mimicked her first tentative caress. His fingertips, her breast, one exhilarating buzz of contact. "Here…or here?"

When he circled her dusky-pink areola with the pad of his thumb, her back arched off the bed. The plump undercurve of her breast caught his retreating hand, searing him with pure, sweet fire as a single word of denial exploded from her lips.

"No?" He didn't believe her, didn't believe he could have been anywhere near her wildly responsive body and not have touched, tasted, taken. "I didn't touch you like that?"

She shook her head, dragging a tress of hair across her throat. Mitch smoothed it back and let his touch linger. Funny how he'd thought her hair cool—cool in the rain, cool in the snow. Now it felt like sun-warmed silk, as fine textured as the smooth stretch of her throat. He bent to kiss that exposed stretch of skin and her low, needy whimper of response rocked him to the core.

"Tell me what you want," he whispered hoarsely. "Because I don't remember."

"I want…want to…"

Her husky attempt at words petered out, but her eyes snapped with hot, restless frustration as she lifted her aroused breasts to brush his bare chest. Oh, man. Jaw clenched, he absorbed that first electric surge of contact without totally losing it. Then he sank a controlled inch lower, enough to feel the full, sizzling impact of skin against skin, soft against hard.

"More?" he asked, rolling his chest against hers in slow-motion torment. "Like this?"

"Like *this*," she countered, drawing the last word into a sexy hiss as she took his hand and dragged it to her breast. As his fingers closed around her supple flesh.

Oh, yes. Exactly like this.

Had she responded so wildly the last time? With those shallow panting breaths at the simple touch of his tongue? Had she clasped his head to her body as he drew her nipple into his mouth? Had she arched her back and gasped when he sank into her wet heat?

Had she screamed his name as she climaxed?

Mitch battled that raw imagery for all of three rapid-fire heartbeats…and lost. He had to know. His hands spanned her rib cage, then slid to her waist. Hunger surged in his blood as his fingertips skimmed her pale feminine curls. Delved deeper.

"Did I touch you here?"

She moistened her bottom lip with her tongue, a stroke of heat Mitch felt in one place most profoundly. It screamed for the touch of that tongue. Hell, that steel-hard part of him screamed, full stop, especially when he parted her woman's folds and found her, wet and hot and ready.

Her eyes widened as if with wonder, and a vague sense of unease snaked through his blood, seeking purchase anywhere not driven by frantic, desperate hunger. *Slow down,* it warned, *think about this.* But then she took his face between her unsteady hands and drew his mouth down to hers, kissing him with all the moist heat he craved, and he was lost.

Stopping, slowing down…not a snowball's chance in hell. He was careering down the mountainside, skating on the brink of control. One more turn and he would be gone, taken, over the edge and screaming toward oblivion. Before then he needed to get naked. And to get protection.

He dragged himself away from the taste of oblivion, dragged himself up from the depths of her sultry eyes. "Please," she whispered. "Please, don't stop."

Mitch smiled tightly. "I doubt that's possible."

"Then, why are you—" Emily stopped midquestion, her concern shifting to wide-eyed awe as he stripped down to bare skin and crossed to the dresser. She swallowed. "Oh."

Watching him open the just-in-case pack and don protection caused her heart to skip jerkily in her chest. *What are you doing, Emily Jane Warner? Who do you think you're fooling with your* please, don't stops? *You are so unprepared for this, so not ready for the consequences.*

But when he turned and started back toward the bed, his sheer magnificence—*everywhere*—silenced that rebellious whisper of trepidation. A wave of emotion rolled through her, an immense and complicated blend of elation and heat and awe and tenderness. Gaze fixed on his, she slipped free of the robe and welcomed him into her arms and her body. For a moment he hesitated, a question burning deep in his eyes, a quiet desperation to know the truth.

Emily whispered the only answer she knew. "Yes."

Yes, I'm ready. Yes, I want you. Yes, I always have and always will.

When he plunged into her body, she tried but couldn't contain her choked cry. He stilled, shock etched all over his face as he—finally—comprehended the extent of her nothing-happened-before assertions. "You're a virgin."

"Was," she corrected, shifting her position experimentally, enjoying the result. Meeting the accusation in his eyes head-on. "I think you've just taken care of that."

She moved again, and so did he, easing deeper as her body adjusted to the new sensation. Mitch inside her body, hot and hard and heavy. What a mind-blowing concept. Her focus hazed with renewed heat as she studied the tightly strained body joined so intimately with hers.

The fine sprinkling of dark hair on his forearms and chest and abdomen. The sheen of highly heated skin, skin stretched taut over powerful muscles that rippled as he drew a breath. The released breath huffing warm air against her skin. Everything entranced her; everything turned her whole being restless with need.

She dragged her short nails down the hard line of his back. "This is nice, but I need to move. I want you to move."

"This—" he ground out between his teeth "—is not nice, sweetheart."

Emily's heart lurched, caught between the joy of that endearment and the notion that he wasn't enjoying himself.

"It's not?"

"Not nice." He licked at her bottom lip. "Exquisite. But I want to take it slow. I don't want to hurt you, Em."

"Slow's nice," she whispered, lifting her hips and wrapping her legs around him, liking the new intimacy and the groan of pleasure it drew from his lips. And he finally started to move, rocking against her in a slow, patient rhythm, thrusting with infinite care and control, as the pressure built low in her belly.

She rolled her head back on the bed when his teeth scraped her nipples, when he drew her into his mouth and sucked with that same exquisite rhythm. Then she felt the scorching stroke of his thumb at her core, and she clutched his shoulders and cried out as he thrust into her more strongly, as the tension gathered and tightened and burst with pleasure. Above her Mitch stiffened and jerked, as deep inside her pulsing body he found his own release.

Too much bath oil and lotion had obviously softened her mind as well as her skin, because Emily had been lying in his bed, her skin still flushed and sensitized, imagining that the sated sighs and tender smiles and who-could-have-known? looks were still to come.

It took all of five minutes, she estimated, for the spell of intimacy to evaporate. For the tension in the hard body at her side to gather and build and tauten until it exploded in one swift, forceful question.

"Why?"

The curt word hit her smack between the eyes like some reality snowball. *Wham. You're it.* She swung her legs over the side of the bed and reached for her discarded robe. Maybe it would halt the chill creeping up her spine and trembling through her limbs, although she seriously doubted it.

At least she would feel less exposed.

While she wrapped herself tightly in its warm folds, she heard movement behind her as if he, too, had reached for his clothes. Her heart shouldn't have dipped with disappointment, had no right to expect more.

"I'm not sure which 'why' you want me to answer," she said carefully, turning the slipknot into a bow with careful, deliberate hands. The action helped control their propensity to shake.

He stilled, the silence in the room complete and intense, until he blew out a breath. "Yeah, well, neither am I."

Surprised, she turned and caught him watching her,

his expression strangely unsure. Vulnerable. For several slow, thudding heartbeats she stared back, the breath aching in her lungs. That look demanded honesty; her heart demanded the same. He'd been so shocked when he entered her body, so… She gave up on the tie and wrapped her arms around herself. "You thought you'd slept with me, didn't you? All this time?"

Yes. The answer burned in his eyes.

"Despite what I told you?" So very many times. *Nothing happened, Mitch.*

"Just for the record," he said slowly, deliberately, "I don't consider undressing you and wrestling you into my bed as nothing."

"Just for the record—" she met his eyes with the same heat and purpose and honesty "—there wasn't any wrestling involved."

"You were in my bed, naked and willing, and nothing happened?" He shook his head. "I'm finding this hard to believe."

"You weren't looking for that kind of relief. Not that night." Memories of his despair licked through her, dark shadowy memories and the specter of his beautiful, accomplished, treacherous wife. How could Emily have misinterpreted so hugely? Sure, he'd sought comfort that night, but what he'd really wanted was his beloved Annabelle. "My misjudgment," she added softly.

"And today? Was this a misjudgment?"

She longed to say no, to tell him she'd just lived her wildest dream. To say that her only misjudgment was in expecting more of the afterward, but she couldn't force the words past her lips. Couldn't keep the conflict of impossible dreams from spilling into her eyes.

"I don't know," she managed eventually, her voice choked with emotion.

"I'm sorry, Em."

Of all the things she didn't want to hear right now, sorry topped the list. "Because I was a virgin?"

"Hell, Em." He scrubbed a hand across his face. "I had no right to sleep with you."

"Because you're my boss? Because you still see me as a child, in your care, in need of your protection?"

"You are in my care—"

"I'm an adult and it's my day off, so forget feeling guilty." Amazing how a little righteous indignation could come to a girl's aid, delivering the strength and the anger to cut through the tears and his attempt to justify. "I wanted this to happen and, yes, my judgment is probably way off, because, God help me, I want it to happen again. And again and again. And if that freaks you out, as my boss, then it's probably best if you don't remain my boss, although that will pain me and Joshua, both."

For a long while her vocal avalanche hung in the air between them. So much passion, so much emotion, and she didn't have the foggiest idea from where it all came. *Liar,* a rogue voice whispered. *It came straight from your heart, direct from that corner of your soul where all your secrets hide.*

"Finished?" he asked with infuriating calm.

Finished but for one last point. "If there's any other reason you feel sorry, I don't want to know." When her eyes started to fill with damn-fool tears again, she knew she had to get out of there. She made it all the way to the door before he stopped her.

"Where are you going?"

Away, anywhere, not here. But she said the first thing that came to mind. "It's time to pick up Joshua."

A beat of silence. "It's your day off."

Of all the comebacks. Emily threw her hands in the air. "Fine, *you* go get him. If we're going to make checkout time, I need to start packing."

Mitch had wanted to keep her there in his bedroom, to challenge most everything she'd said, to tackle the things left unsaid. But how could he have stopped her determined path to the door? By physically blocking her path, making her meet his eyes, putting his hands on her?

Not a good idea.

Not with the heat of her passionate words still simmering in the air. Not with edited highlights burning through his blood. *I want it to happen again. And again and again.* Definitely not while the gleam of tears in her big cinnamon eyes shaped that heat with a myriad of new and unsettling facets. More than six hours later that memory still turned him inside out.

His hands tightened on the SUV's steering wheel, but he kept his eyes fixed on the road. Why hazard a sideways look? He knew she sat stiff and straight in the passenger seat...and not because of any driving fears. Tension might as well have climbed aboard this trip and strapped itself into a spare seat, it loomed so large and real and palpable.

Well, hell, he'd needed time to think, to assess everything that was right about what had happened in that mountain bedroom, and all that was wrong. He'd needed time to find a solution, one that compensated his lack of restraint, his refusal to accept her word, his failure to honor the most basic of boss-employee ethics.

Mostly he needed to prevent her leaving.

One solution grabbed ahold of his brain, strong and unshakable. A full afternoon of his son's exuberance, a plane trip back to Sydney and an hour on the road back to Plenty hadn't loosened its hold. A perfect, workable solution for a range of practical reasons that had nothing to do with Emily in his bed, again and again and again.

A glance in the rearview mirror confirmed that Joshua had finally succumbed to exhaustion. Beside him Emily sat constrained by a seat belt and the confines of a vehicle speeding through the darkening landscape. No means of escape. He cleared his throat.

"What you said back there, at the lodge…"

Mitch sensed as much as saw her straighten, stiffen. "Which particular piece? I seem to recall saying rather a lot."

"You mentioned leaving…if what you said freaked me out."

The pause was only a heartbeat, but that beat reverberated through the car like a drum roll. "And did it? Freak you out?"

"The thought of you leaving does." Hand over hand, he steadied the car around a tight right-hand bend before he could slant her a look. She sat staring straight ahead, her hands gripping the edges of her seat as if to anchor her there. Smart choice, he thought wryly, as his own stomach jumped with nerves. "I think we should get married."

Ten

A car seat, it turned out, did not provide ample mooring when the world spun out from under oneself. Emily dug her fingers deeper into the upholstery but reality continued to whirl with the shock of Mitch's…did you call that out-of-nowhere statement a proposal?

"Are you serious?" she asked. After the devastating end to his previous marriage… "You want to get married again?"

"I want to do the right thing. For Joshua and for you."

Of course he didn't want to get married. He wanted "to do the right thing," for everyone else but himself. Emily shook her head and, paradoxically, it stopped spinning. "Because you slept with me? Because of some misplaced sense of responsibility? That is so old-fashioned it's laughable."

He didn't laugh.

"I mean, it's not even as if you might *have to* marry me, seeing as we used protection."

"So did my sisters," he said shortly. "And look at them."

Both pregnant when they married. Emily's heart stuttered at the possibility that her one explosive, mind-blowing sexual experience could yield a similar result. *No,* she cautioned herself sharply. Not even a slim, next-to-nothing possibility—she had never been that lucky.

"Even if the impossible happened," she said, faking a light tone as best she could. "I don't have any shotgun-toting relatives who are likely to track you down."

"Exactly. You don't have any relatives who help you out at any turn. They didn't even know where you'd gone, how to find you, when you disappeared. I didn't know where you were, in what condition."

"You thought that I might be…?" Lord. No wonder he'd been so incensed by her disappearance, so grim that first night on Gramps's verandah. So insistent about unearthing the truth.

He huffed out a breath. "The thought did cross my mind. More than once."

"I didn't know you thought we'd even…"

Her vague, waving gesture from her to him and back again, wrung a dry humorless laugh from Mitch. "Done it? Hell, Emily, I couldn't even remember what we'd done or not done, so what was the chance I'd have thought to use protection?"

"I didn't know." *Any of that. Anything.* Her voice trailed off as she slumped back in her seat, shell-shocked by the notion that he'd thought she may have been pregnant. *With his baby.* Her hand shifted, hovering over her belly as her heart and her stomach and her emotions jumped all over the place.

"Why did you leave?" he asked, then before she could begin to think how to answer that pearler, he made an impatient sound low in his throat. "No, you didn't just leave, you dropped off the face of the earth. Obviously—since we didn't do anything—you had no concerns about an unwanted baby, so why, Emily?"

Emily pressed a hand to her jittery stomach. What could she say? I ran because we *didn't* do it? Because, even with you falling-down drunk, I couldn't seduce you, so what chance I could ever win your love? Reflexively she pressed her hand against the ache low in her stomach. "If there had been any chance of a baby, I wouldn't have hidden it from you," she said honestly. "A child needs as many parents to love her as possible."

For a second she felt his eyes on her—silent, watchful, measuring—and then he needed to concentrate on the road as it wound its way over the top of the Great Divide. Hopefully she'd diverted him from the why-did-you-leave issue, although her whole body tensed in expectation of the next twist and turn.

"You haven't had much of that in your life," he observed, his voice low and unhurried.

Emily frowned. "That's not what I meant. It was like a hypothetical—if I ever found myself in that position."

"Based on your own childhood." Not a question, although he held up a hand in case she chose to object. "Home's important to you? And family?"

The aching tension shifted higher, circling her chest

in a steel-banded embrace. "I'm not exactly your expert on home and family."

"Is that why you chose nannying as a career? Because that's what you wanted?"

Wanted? Ah, Mitch, that word doesn't even begin to describe how much I have craved, yearned, wished-upon-a-candled-cake for those things. "I suppose you could say that," she prevaricated. "Except the home-slash-family isn't really yours when you're the nanny. It's only a loaner."

"I'm giving you the chance to change that," he said. "All you have to do is marry me."

Her heart was already starting to pound when she met his eyes. Only a brief clash before his returned to the road, but the steely purpose, the dark intensity…she dragged in a serrated breath and felt the tremor roll right through her—a tremor that whispered with insidious and seductive intent.

Marry him, Emily, and you can have it all.

"That sounds too easy." Like one of those unsolicited lottery letters: Congratulations! You are the one in ten-million winner! The kind you toss straight in the garbage because you know there's a catch. "I get a home and a family, but what do you get, Mitch?"

The look he slanted her—one brief second—sizzled with all they'd shared that afternoon. Her mouth may well have fallen open, her eyes definitely clouded with heat, and her thighs tingled from that one blazing glimpse of what marriage to Mitch would include. Hot and powerful and often. She closed her mouth before she said something ill-advised, such as, Yes, I'll marry you.

"Don't underestimate the power of great sex," he

said softly. Only a tiny hint of humor edged his deep velvet-cream drawl. "Especially when it's been a while."

Emily swallowed, caught between powerful flattery and cynical reality. Sure, he may use the "great" adjective, but if it had been "a while"—and how long constituted a while for a man like Mitch?—then any sex might qualify. She looked at him now, with those darkly rugged good looks, his athlete's body, and that deceptive calm she knew could explode into heated passion at the drop of a...bathrobe...and she shook her head. "That's not something you would have to marry to get regularly, Mitch. I imagine you'd only have to crook a finger at certain parties or bars."

Something hardened in his profile. "I'm not interested in picking up my next wife at a bar."

Annabelle, the beautiful party girl. How could she have forgotten? All the shimmering heat of sexual flattery faded, leaving only hard reality. He's suggested they marry—what was the catch? "Do you think, honestly, that I qualify as your next wife?"

"You're a good person, Emily, easy to be around. You're warm, practical, even-tempered...usually," he added with a quirk of his lips.

"You left out plain." And vanilla, her own personal favorite descriptor.

Strangely enough, Mitch's eyes sparked. "I've seen you naked, Emily. You're far from plain."

Oh. Okay. She swallowed.

"But that's not the point." His gaze switched back to the road. "I like your company. We could have a pretty decent marriage."

Pretty decent, good, practical—what happened to great sex and her far-from-plain naked body?

"Sounds like good grounds for a friendship," she said.

"Maybe that's what I want this time, a relationship without all the emotional upheavals. Where I'm not walking around on eggshells struggling to understand what could have gone wrong and backpedaling like crazy to make up for whatever damn thing I messed up."

And there it was, his first marriage summarized in one heated string of words. Not that Emily should have been surprised—she'd lived through two years of Annabelle's emotional dramas—but, oh, what she'd give to inspire that kind of high passion. And she knew, suddenly, that she didn't care for a "pretty decent" marriage, and she definitely couldn't guarantee a lack of emotional upheaval. Her emotions were heaving all over the place at this very moment.

"I'm sorry," she said softly. And her mouth twisted a little with the irony of what she was doing, saying, turning down—her fantasy for most of the past three years. "But I don't think I can marry you."

He huffed out a breath that sounded both bitter and disbelieving. "Sorry? Why are you sorry?"

"For a lot of things." Mostly that he'd started this whole circular conversation with *I think we should get married* instead of *I want to get married.* That he wanted a clear conscience and a nanny who wouldn't leave rather than a wife who loved him. "I can't be the kind of wife you're looking for."

"Don't you think I'm the best judge of that?" His quiet words wrapped her in a tempting cloak. "Promise me you'll think about it. Will you do that?"

In all honesty… "Yes." Her answer was a thin whisper of sound, barely audible over the road noise.

Of course she would think about it. Quite possibly for the rest of her life.

Amazingly, Emily slept. She didn't remember nodding off but she woke with a start that jerked her head upright. Where were they? She squinted through her side window toward a single light glowing in the darkness. A farmyard, she thought, although one she didn't recognize.

"Are we home yet?" Joshua asked groggily from the back seat. When she turned to see him rubbing his eyes, several pieces of his hair standing on end and a just-woke-up pout on his little mouth, she felt the same winded punch as when she'd hit the ground hard that first day on skis.

"Soon, honey."

Through the back window she saw Mitch coming toward them, a dark silhouette whose size and presence blocked out much of that one bright spotlight. The ache in her chest intensified. Did she really think she could resist such a twosome? Couldn't she simply take what she could get, and hang the grand passion?

"Where's Daddy?"

"He's coming now," she told Joshua, a smile starting as she recognized the squirming bundle under his arm. "Looks as if we stopped to pick up a passenger."

The back door opened and Joshua yelled "Digger!" and greeted his pal as if they'd been apart weeks instead of days. By the dog's clamorous response, the elation was mutual.

Laughing, she turned back around to find Mitch sliding into the driver's seat and watching her with a strange expression on his face. Her laughter faded.

Those new, shorter layers of hair were probably standing on end like Joshua's. Self-conscious, she finger combed them back into place. "Better?" she asked.

He shook his head—no answer at all—then Joshua asked, "How come Digger was here? We left him with Uncle Quade."

"It appears your uncle Quade got busy." Warmth and a subtle sense of contained excitement turned his lopsided grin into a thing of powerful beauty. For a moment it blinded Emily to everything, including the cell phone he brandished.

"The baby?" she squeaked.

"He texted to say we'd find Digger down here with the Andersons."

Emily rocked forward impatiently, grabbing hold of his jacket sleeve. "Forget the dog. Have they gone to the hospital? Has Chantal had the baby?"

His grin widened. "Seems like."

Charlotte Quade made her entrance into the world several hours before their return from the ski trip. Just like her cousin Bridie, she jumped the gun by almost a month, impatient to get out and start bossing everyone around, Mitch surmised.

Emily smiled, remembering. How long since she'd seen him so...happy. Charlotte's safe arrival completely overshadowed the tension that still resonated between them, that would continue to resonate until she made a decision about her future.

Would she change her mind? Could she marry him?

Frankly, she didn't know. There had been times in the last two days when he could have taken her by the hand and led her to the nearest celebrant. Talk about your complete family joyfest! Emily caught the overflow and let it fill every hollow ache in her soul until she practically vibrated with longing. Her smile turned wry. So much for staying strong.

"Good to see you smiling," Mitch said, steering the SUV she'd yet to drive into the hospital parking lot. "All the way in here, you looked tense enough to snap."

Well, yes, but she had justification. For a start, this was her first visit with Chantal, and the prospect of seeing baby Charlotte filled her with a complicated mix of anticipation and excitement and dread. With Mitch alongside and all that my-sisters-used-protection-and-look-at-them talk whispering away in the back of her consciousness—Lord help her if she got to actually hold this infant.

Secondly, Mitch's parents had arrived home this morning and although she'd met them many times in the past, that was before she'd slept with their son and agreed to consider his marriage suggestion. Which kind of put a new spin on the meeting, her nerves had decided as she'd dithered over her wardrobe choice.

In the end she'd gone with her nice, plain, practical and only skirt. With nervous hands she smoothed the woolen fabric over her knees and felt it prickle against her bare skin. She had managed to stick a finger right through her only pair of pantyhose while dressing. When she felt Mitch's gaze track her nervous smoothing, sensual warmth rippled through her blood. Just from that one, covert glance. Lord, she had it bad.

"I've got your present, Em," Joshua crowed, unsnapping his seat belt and reaching for his car door the second they stopped. "Come on, I know where we go. I'll show you."

Slowing him from a gallop to something resembling a walk, and responding to his excited chatter, kept her mind and her nerves occupied all the way to Chantal's room—except for that moment when she'd caught their reflection in the plate-glass entrance doors. Mitch looked so tall and broad and handsome; she looked not so bad in her off-white sweater and crimson skirt; Joshua strode, confident and happy, with his arms clutching the gift-wrapped parcel.

A family, she'd thought with a sudden shock of discovery. They actually looked like a family.

Then Joshua grabbed her hand and demanded an answer to some pressing problem, but she stored that image in the back of her mind for later…later, when she would pore over all the carefully filed information and make her decision. But now—she paused on the threshold and inhaled deeply—now she had other Goodwins to deal with.

"Come on, Emmy." Joshua tugged on her hand, pulling her into a large, airy room that could not have contained any more flowers or balloons or pink stuffed animals without extensive remodeling. It was also surprisingly light on people. No Goodwins senior, just Chantal and Quade and Julia, the latter holding a tiny, swaddled pink bundle.

"I got another present 'cept this one's from Emmy." Joshua plonked it down on the bed. "It's a bear for Charlie."

"Charlotte," at least two voices corrected.

"Told you so." Julia sounded very pleased with herself.

"All Charlottes do not get called Charlie," Chantal

said tartly, and, as always when Goodwins gathered, the room soon spun with teasing and laughter and it was so easy to relax and feel a part of it. Emily released her pent-up anxiety in a big smile and an even bigger hug for each of the new parents. When Joshua asked for a turn holding the baby, she instinctively hunkered down to help.

"Hold her so," she instructed softly, helping cradle the tiny bonneted head. She was so delicate and pink and sweet smelling and perfect. "Isn't she beautiful?"

"For a girl," Joshua decided with a heavy sigh. "Can the next baby be a boy?"

Julia patted him on the head and promised, "We'll do our best, sweetie," which drew a shudder from Chantal. "Do not even mention 'next baby' in my company." But Quade squeezed her hand, and the look that passed between them was so full of love it turned Emily to mush. She figured there would be more Quade babies, God willing.

"I have to scoot," Julia said. "Or my little princess will be spoiled beyond redemption by the grands. You should see all the presents they bought in London."

The *P* word captured Joshua's attention. "Is there any for me?"

"What do you think?"

His grin spread like spilled sunshine. "Nan and Da always bring me presents."

Julia cocked a brow at Mitch. "Okay if I take him around to visit with them?"

And in the ensuing organization of who-was-going-where-and-for-how-long, followed by the many kisses and hugs of departure, Emily ended up holding the baby. As she settled Charlotte's insubstantial weight in her arms, as she gazed into her sleeping face with its perfect cupid's-bow mouth and brow scrunched as if in concentrated thought, all the peripheral chatter faded away. Need, want, longing closed around her like a physical entity—a many-tentacled, living, breathing, writhing thing that threatened to squeeze everything else from her soul.

You can have this, Emily, your own tiny piece of God's perfection.

She looked up then, looked up to find Mitch watching her, seeing her most-secret craving written all over her face. Somewhere deep inside she felt a twang of alarm. *You're handing him everything he needs,* it warned her, *every tool he needs to shape your decision.* But she could not do a thing about it. In that moment, she could not even bring herself to care.

"I'm sorry I missed your parents."

"No you're not." From the corner of his eye—eyes he needed to keep fixed on the road and the evening traffic in midtown Cliffton—Mitch saw her turn to look at him, surprised by his response. "You were nervous as hell about seeing them."

She didn't answer but she didn't have to. Her fidgety hands gave her away, first smoothing the skirt over her thighs, then tucking it beneath them. If she kept doing that, he wouldn't be able to help himself. He'd give in to the impulse to untuck, to unsmooth, to slide his hand under that prim good-girl skirt to touch the soft, warm flesh beneath.

"Are we going there now? To pick up Joshua?"

"No." One corner of his mouth kicked into a slow grin. "He won't be halfway through opening those presents."

"Oh."

Signaling his intent, he turned the SUV at the lights, onto the road leading home.

"Didn't you love the blanket they brought for Charlotte? It was so soft and pink—" She laughed self-consciously. "And I'm sure you didn't even notice."

"I noticed."

He'd noticed the tender skill of her hands as they held the soft, pink-blanketed bundle. He'd noticed the captivated stillness of her body, then the flood of rapture as she settled into the chair with Charlie in her arms. Cradled against her breast.

And he knew in those first ten seconds what it would take to change her mind about marrying him. Not the security of a permanent home or—what had she called it that night in the car? A loaner family. Right. Even with a wedding band on her finger, that's how she would see them. Unless she had a family of her own.

She would marry him for that.

Disquiet stirred deep in his gut, a cautionary edge that he quickly kyboshed. So what if she didn't want to marry *him,* if she was more interested in what he could give her? It wasn't as if he'd offered much of himself in this bargain. It wasn't as if he had much of himself to offer. But he did want to marry her, for all their sakes. For Joshua's need of a mother, for Emily's need of a family, for the guilty edges of his conscience.

This marriage was an arrangement where they all could have what they wanted, and he intended to make it so. Whatever it took.

"Have you made up your mind?" he asked, flicking on the headlights as they cleared the city limits and headed into the countryside.

"I'm...no." Her exhalation sounded harried. "Please don't push me right now."

In the tricky twilight he couldn't see her eyes, but he pictured them dark and uneasy and pleading. "Okay," he said.

"You won't push me for an answer?" she asked, suspicious.

"Not right now." He could wait another twenty minutes, until they were home, and then all bets were off. He intended to push for as long as it took to get the answer he wanted.

"Should I be worried?" she asked with a nervous little laugh. "About later?"

Mitch smiled in the gathering darkness. "Very."

Eleven

He took her hand as they walked from the garage to the house, and Emily didn't object. Too nice, the roughness of his man's skin and the warm strength of his grip as his fingers curled around hers. At some point—possibly when they brushed shoulders walking up the verandah steps—she was struck by a strange sense of first-date awkwardness. Probably because she had never held hands with a man before. Weird to feel nervous when she'd done so much more, when she was pretty certain they were about to do it all over again.

Still, when he opened the front door and led her inside, a nervous shiver coursed through her body. His grip tightened and he pulled her around to face him in the silent darkness of the entry hall. "Worried yet?" he asked, and her pulse jumped.

"Very."

He laughed low in his throat, a husky rumble that hummed through her senses. Then he lifted her hand and pressed a series of soft kisses into her palm, her wrist, the pad of her thumb, and the humming grew shrill, rhythmic. Exactly like the ringing of a phone. Intent on seducing her one nibbling kiss at a time, Mitch either didn't notice or didn't care.

"Aren't you going to get that?" she asked, her voice hitching as the tip of his tongue traced a line across her palm. Probably her heart line.

"You want me to?"

Did she want to stop breathing? "No, but it might be your parents. Joshua."

The warm breath of his sigh sloughed her kiss-dampened skin, but he straightened at that magic word *Joshua* and turned toward the still-ringing phone. He did not let go of her hand, however, towing Emily in his wake as he strode to his office and circled his huge leather office chair to pick up the receiver. With his other hand.

Eyes on hers, he tugged her forward, slowly, inexorably, until she bumped into his legs. The inside of his thighs, actually, since he had rested back against his desk, knees spread wide enough to accommodate her body. For a brief second she closed her eyes and indulged in his nearness—the hard heat of his thighs, the scents of winter and leather and man, a few rumbled words into the phone.

The phone. Her eyes shot open to find herself looking right into his, so green and hot and steady that she forgot her place again. He took her hand—the one clasped so firmly in his—and put it on his thigh, holding it there with the same steady insistence she saw in his gaze.

I want your hand on me, was the message she read there.

"That's right," he murmured.

To the unknown caller or to her? She didn't have time to decide as the pressure of his hand increased, spreading her fingers over the hard muscle beneath. How would this feel without the denim, with only his hair-roughened skin under her palm? The breath she drew felt shallow, edgy, catching in the constricted heat of her throat as she imagined peeling those jeans down his legs and touching him in all the ways and places she had fantasized.

"That's fine with me." The husky note to his voice and the crooked edge to his grin caused her pulse to flutter madly. Could he read her mind? Possibly. Because his hand encouraged hers, moving higher on a pulse-hammering journey of discovery. When she discovered the distended fly of his jeans, a flush started deep in her belly and spread through her blood. One brow arched wickedly as he said, "I have things to do."

So it seemed. Under her fingers his arousal pulsed; his eyes blazed with a matching fervor, and his hands…his hot, rough-skinned, sneaky hands were on her bare thighs. She snapped to attention. *Both* his hands were on her thighs, which meant she was cupping him all by her wanton self, and the telephone receiver lay discarded on the desk.

"Joshua's fine," he said in short explanation. "He's sleeping over."

She snatched her hand away. "*That was your mother?* While I had my hand…" She couldn't finish the thought, let alone the question. She couldn't do anything but slump forward, hands clasping her flaming cheeks.

"It was Julia, actually. And as perceptive as my sister is, I doubt she knows where your hand—"

"*I* know," she fired back, inflamed by the soft laughter in his voice. "And *you* knew, yet you didn't do a thing to stop me."

"I didn't want to stop you." His eyes glinted, this time with more than teasing amusement. "I don't want you to stop."

"Well, I think the mood might be effectively snuffed," she said, her pulse and her voice leaping in gazelle-like unison as his hands stroked the back of her thighs.

"Are you sure?" His touch gentled, a sensual whisper of a caress. Then paused. "Did you wear this skirt on account of my parents?"

Emily tried to duck away. There seemed something inherently wrong with wearing a prim-and-proper skirt to meet a man's parents, then letting him put his hand up it. That hand now conspired with his thighs to prevent her escape, holding her firmly and securely in place. Talk about being trapped between a rock and a hard place.

"You look very nice, Emily. I'm sure my parents would have been impressed, although—" his hand glided smoothly over her bare skin "—no panty hose?"

"It's not what you think," she said quickly, flushing from the inside out. "I only had one pair and they laddered when I put them on, and with the boots and the length of the skirt, I didn't think anyone would notice."

"I'm noticing. And just so you know, I hate the damn things."

Emily swallowed. And struggled to understand what, exactly, he hated because his hands were cupping her bottom, then dipping under the waistband of her panties, then… She sucked in a startled breath. "What are you doing?"

"Taking your pants off," he said, so matter-of-factly that a surprised note of laughter burst from her lips.

"Do you hate *all* underwear?" she asked as hers shimmied down her legs. When they caught on her knee-high boots, what could she do but kick them off?

"At the moment—" and she felt the shockingly cool caress of night air as he bunched her skirt higher "—that would be a yes."

Their eyes met as he clasped her bared buttocks, his hands a hot, solid contrast to the tremor that shivered through her body. And his eyes! They glittered with purpose, with knowledge, with power. Oh, yes, he knew what he was about, seducing her for his own means, to influence her decision. He knew, and Emily strived to formulate an objection as his hands slid down, parting her legs, dipping inward in a delicious probing caress.

"Are you trying to manipulate me?" she managed huskily.

"I think that's what I am doing."

In the literal sense of the word, yes. Those hands, those fingers. Weak-kneed, she shook her head.

"You want me to stop?" he asked, stopping.

Heaven help her, no, but she forced herself to focus. To grab a brief moment of sanity while she still could. "I want you to promise not to ask for a marriage answer while you're touching me. Anywhere. In any way.''

''I won't ask, Emily.''

He looked into her eyes and he gave his word and she believed him. She believed him, too, when he hauled her closer and nuzzled his face against her neck and muttered, ''I want to taste you,'' against her flushed skin.

Emily smiled. ''I don't have any problem with that.''

But he ignored her proffered lips, standing and reversing their positions so quickly her head spun. When her perspective steadied, she found herself perched on the edge of his desk with her legs spread and her skirt shucked up around her waist, and Mitch looking down at her with hot, hungry eyes.

She tried to cover up; he didn't let her. ''Lean back,'' he directed as his hands skimmed her inner thighs. ''On your elbows.''

Her lids fluttered shut and she jittered with a mix of nerves and need when his fingers parted her, when he touched her with tenderness and skill in that place so moist and wanting. His thumb rasped against her sensitive flesh, once, twice, and he murmured one word. ''Beautiful.''

The last of her self-consciousness evaporated and she let him spread her thighs wider, felt them tremble weakly as the silky coolness of his hair brushed their inner skin. Then his mouth was on her and the first velvet rasp of his tongue lifted her off the desk.

Approval hummed in his voice as he soothed her back down. ''Easy, sweetheart, I'm only just starting.''

''You're only—'' The interplay of mouth and fingers drove the rest of that thought from her mind. Awash with heat, with building pleasure, with an unbearable intensity like a spring coiling tighter and tighter inside her womb, she grabbed for purchase. Her fingers tunneled into his hair and held on tight.

"Please, Mitch, you have to... have to—" *Stop, keep going—no, stop.* She craved his heat and fullness inside her but before she could tell him, show him, beg him, her release came in a blinding wave of sensation that left her limp and trembling. Even as she felt him move away, she could not move to save herself, to cover herself, to do any more than slump back with a long growl of wonder.

Mitch had never heard anything more erotic than that sound. It ricocheted through him, rebounding off every steel-hard facet until he had to grit his teeth and fist his hands to control the urgent, pulsing need to unzip his jeans and bury his most steel-hard facet in her soft body. He wouldn't last a minute, and that wasn't nearly long enough.

He aimed to give her incredible, amazing, earthshattering. He wouldn't ask any questions, but he aimed to wring so many yeses from her soft lips that she forgot the meaning of no. He needed to last a lot longer than one hot, frantic, pulsing minute.

Looking didn't help his tenuous control any. Not in her current pose, spread out before him in her good-girl clothes and a pair of black boots that looked blood-thumping bad.

"All right?" he asked, trusting himself—barely— to brush his knuckles over her knee. Her thigh.

"I think so. That was..."

"Don't you dare say nice."

"Sort of spectacular," she finished, her brown eyes luminous with wonder. Another first-time experience.

The strength of his primitive, possessive response—*he was first, she was his!*—rocked him to the core. His hands closed over her knees. He leaned in close. "Only *sort of?*"

"It felt a little one-sided." She moistened her lips. "As if something was miss—"

Mitch agreed. He kissed her long and hard, his hands on her hips, her back, supporting her, holding her, dragging her forward and up against the thick pulse of his erection. *The missing something?* Hell, he'd missed this mouth, so sweet and hot and giving. And her breasts. He'd been too eager—he needed to see, to touch.

With his mouth still on hers, he unhooked her bra and felt the needy quiver of her lips. He couldn't stop himself plunging his tongue into her mouth and grinding his hips against hers, wishing his jeans gone. Wanting to be inside her everywhere. "I don't have enough hands," he muttered, relinquishing her lips to tug the sweater over her head.

And Emily—his practical, helpful, intuitive Emily—came to his aid, ridding him of his sweater and unbuttoning his shirt and jeans because his hands were full of her luscious breasts. Then her hands were full of him, and the strength of his response punched a guttural groan from his throat. Too good. "Not good," he ground out.

Her desire-hazed eyes turned hesitant. "Did I hurt you? Sorry, I—"

"No, God no." He shook his head and pressed a kiss to her mouth. A second. "Just risky, given my current state."

And she insisted on checking out his meaning with an inquisitive, heavy-lidded gaze and the gentlest stroke of one fingertip across the head of his need. She was killing him. He had no hope of regaining control, of waiting, of prolonging.

Of remembering his purpose.

Hands under her knees, he hauled her to the very edge of the desk. Her fingers curled into the taut muscles of his buttocks, and he felt the erotic slide of her dampness. Her spectacular, extravagant, welcoming heat. "Is this risky, too?" she asked.

A scant breath away from plunging, he remembered what this was about—this risk, precisely—and he couldn't do it. "I don't have protection."

"Oh." She swallowed. "Do you want to go and get some?"

"Your choice."

Wistful wanting softened the desire in her eyes, a glancing hint of all he'd seen in her expression when she'd held Chantal's baby. She knew—yeah, she knew—the choice she was making, yet she barely paused, barely blinked, before lifting her knees and hugging his hips with her thighs.

He'd promised not to ask, so he didn't. He told her, "You are going to marry me."

"Yes."

Her answer screamed through him as he sank into her heat, all the way home in one powerful thrust. For a long moment he didn't move, couldn't move, as the sensation of lodging in her slick, tight embrace blew his mind.

It's the complete nakedness, he reasoned as a wave of terrifyingly raw emotion shuddered through him.

The forgotten sensation of skin to most sensitive skin, that's all.

But he could not reason away the knowledge that glowed in her dark eyes as he started to move inside her, in long, powerful, driving strokes. It transcended pleasure, transcended sexual release and tapped into his primitive, male drive. Procreation: the chance that this joining could result in a new life. That knowledge arced between them and thundered in his blood, a thick pulsing rhythm that drove him on without any thought for control, without any desire to hold back.

On some other plane he felt the bite of her short nails and tasted sweat on her skin as he kissed her throat and her breasts and marked her as his mate. When he drew one hard-tipped nipple into his mouth and sucked strongly, her body arched and lifted. She cried out, dragging him with her as shudder after fierce shudder racked their joined bodies.

Mitch's climax exploded with white-hot intensity, splintering him with shards of elation and atonement and rightness and—as he wrapped her lax body in his arms and carried her to his bed—an intense possessive desire to never let her go.

Emily woke late the next morning, relaxed, hungry—no, starving!—and alone. The last left her torn. On the one hand, she appreciated the opportunity to stretch and wince and then hug herself with a big, feel-good smile all over her face. On the other hand, she was…alone. And after the most personal sharing experience of her life, that didn't feel quite right.

So, okay, more than a tiny corner of her heart craved that warm, intimate morning-after togetherness she'd fantasized about the first time, and maybe somewhere in the future they would experience that, she and her husband. Her tummy turned over as she applied that alien label, and again—with an extra twist—at the recollection of how they'd consummated her yes to his proposal. In all ways, the truest sense of the word.

Not right, Emily Jane, a tiny voice warned, but she shoved it aside along with the bedclothes. Sure, he'd had seduction on his mind, to get the answer he wanted, but she'd been the most willing of participants. After holding baby Charlotte, her mind had made itself up. The anxiety attack in the car coming home had been nerves, a natural response to the huge decision already made but not yet spoken. And they'd both agreed on the no-condom issue—there'd been no arm twisting, no pressure, no subterfuge.

"So there," she told that little worrywart voice of conscience. "You can shut the heck up!" Because she was still Joshua's nanny and late for work. Her clothes, she guessed, remained strewn over the office floor, so she grabbed the lengthiest sweater she could find in Mitch's closet and pulled it over her head.

Heart racing, she tapped on the office door, then pushed it open a crack. Mitch—her future husband, she thought, this time with a warm flutter of pleasure—sat in the big office chair with his back to the door, and he held up a hand in a be-with-you-in-a-tick gesture. The warm flutter stilled and cooled. Apparently, this was another morning at work, same as any other, no big deal.

Okay, Emily Jane, you can do this, too. A marriage without emotional upheaval, featuring her good, practical, even-tempered self. A pleasant smile, a nice good-morning, grab your clothes, get out of here.

Her clothes sat in a neatish pile on the spare chair—Mitch must have gathered them up, although she couldn't quite put that picture together. The scene from last night, however, loomed large and detailed in her mind's eye. Her sweater atop the computer monitor, her panties and skirt pooled on the floor where they'd dropped, and her bra...she didn't even recall losing.

Warmth flushed her cheeks as she pushed up the dangling sleeves of her borrowed sweater and crossed to the chair. "I won't disturb you," she began with a crispness she in no way resembled. "Seeing as you're working. I'll just grab my things and leave you be."

But when she bent to pick them up, heat tingled up her spine. She straightened to find Mitch had turned his chair enough to watch. By the angle of his head and that telling tingle, she knew exactly what he'd been watching.

The idea was so much more appealing than his no-greeting greeting, that a big smile spread across her face. "Sorry if I'm interrupting."

"I wasn't working," he said evenly.

Good. Excellent, in fact. Ridiculously pleased, she hugged her clothes to her chest. "Me, neither, and it's after nine. You should have woken me."

"I thought about it...but I had things to do."

Emily recalled the last time he'd used that things-to-do phrase, just before he hung up on Julia last night. Predictably she turned a little jelly-kneed. Then she wondered if he'd thought about waking her as he'd done in the middle of the night, after they'd slept with their bodies spooned in cozy harmony. With his big hands stroking her breasts and his teeth grazing her ear and his—

"I called my in-laws' lawyer," he said, shattering her sensual reverie.

"The Blaineys?" she asked stupidly. Well, of course the Blaineys. Did he have any other in-laws, current or ex?

"I made an appointment for next Tuesday afternoon, late. In Sydney."

"Will Randall and Janet be there?" With exaggerated care, she sat down in the chair. "Have you spoken to them?"

"Not personally but their lawyer will. It's their choice, but this meeting isn't about visitation, so who knows?" He shrugged tightly.

"Are you taking Joshua, then?"

"No. He can stay with my parents while we're gone." He swung back to his computer, suddenly all business. "I thought it a good opportunity, since I'm going to Sydney, to find a convenient registry office and get the marriage paperwork under way. You have a birth certificate?"

She opened her mouth, closed it again, shook her head.

Mitch frowned. "Are you all right?"

"It's just…my head's still spinning from last night, and now you're asking me about registry offices and birth certificates?" She lifted her hands and let them drop, unsure what bothered her most. His cool, remote tone, yes. The unsettling speed, yes. Was he afraid she may still run away? Or did he just want to get it over with so he could resume normal programming?

"There's a thirty-day notice requirement," he said. "It requires both our signatures and the celebrant's so we need to decide where we're getting married before we can lodge it.''

"Decide where...?'' Laughter, inappropriate and borderline hysterical, bubbled up inside, but one glance at her husband-to-be's darkening frown killed the impulse. "I've barely decided that I *am* getting married. I haven't spent a whole lot of time thinking about *where*.''

"A registry office is the best bet. We should be able to get an appointment for as soon as the thirty days are up.''

Emily knew better than to wish for a romantic ceremony with all the traditional trappings, but an appointment sounded so cold and clinical. So unemotional...just like the marriage Mitch wanted. Despite the bundle of clothing hugged against her chest, she couldn't prevent a chill from crawling over her skin. She sucked in a ragged breath, let it out on a shaky laugh. "Is there a need for such a rush? I need to think about this registry office thing.''

"You want a church wedding?''

"No, I just...'' Her voice trailed off as she looked up into his face. "I was only thinking that local might be nicer than Sydney.''

"So every man and his dog can line up outside to stare at you, to wonder why you've gotten married so fast? Is that what you want?''

"That wouldn't bother me,'' she said candidly.

When the day came, she would notice one thing only—this man she was marrying. Everything else would fade into the background as long as he stood waiting to take her hand, to have and to hold and never let go. And as quickly as that thought tiptoed across her mind, the imagery snapped into focus like a page from her wedding album.

She could smell the rosebud buttonhole in his suit jacket; she could see the smattering of dark hair on the back of the hand that reached to take hers; she could feel her throat clog with choking, sentimental tears.

Unfortunately the last wasn't only in her mind's eyes, and she jumped to her feet, casting around for a valid excuse to get the blazes out of there before she succumbed to her emotions. "I'll think about it, okay? Right now I have to go collect Joshua. You said ten-thirty, right?"

He stared back at her a moment, his expression scarily unreadable. Emily had to dig her bare toes into the carpet to stop herself fleeing. She knew—as sure as she stood here wearing nothing but a man's sweater—she would hate whatever he was about to say.

"Why don't we both go," he suggested in a tone that wasn't a suggestion at all. "We can go into Clifton first and look at some rings."

Rings? As in engagement rings? As in symbols of the unbroken circle of love?

Emily didn't realize that her body had gone slack in shocked response, until the clothes she'd clutched so tightly fell to the floor. For a moment she stared at them stupidly, her skirt and sweater and underclothes spread out in stark counterpoint against the muted beige carpet, and then she ducked down to pick them up.

Apparently Mitch had the same idea, because they ended up at opposite ends of her bra in a gentle tug-of-war. She let go and slumped back onto her haunches.

"Don't you want a ring?" he asked.

Confused, unsure, Emily shook her head. She didn't know what she wanted except for all this to be…different. Meaningful. "I think that's something else I need to think about," she said quietly.

For a second he said nothing, but she felt him watching her, probably trying to work out what had happened to that practical, emotionally even creature he thought her to be.

"I'd like you to wear my ring," he said finally, and her gaze leaped to his. "So please do think about it."

"I will."

"And in the meantime—" his eyes, she noticed, were no longer cool, no longer intent on the business of this deal "—I notice you're wearing my sweater."

Emily swallowed. "You don't like it on me?"

"I'd prefer it off you." Heat arced between them. "Come over here."

Emily knew that succumbing to the heat and the desire would not resolve anything. She even suspected he might use the moment to twist her arm about rings and registry offices. But as she inched across the carpet toward him, as she rested her hands on his knees and used the purchase to pull herself into his arms, she told herself it didn't matter.

She was marrying the man she loved, he was offering her the family she craved, so did it really matter how or where they said their vows?

Twelve

"Is the ring not comfortable?" Mitch gestured toward Emily's hand and the solitaire diamond she'd been twisting and turning on her finger ever since he put it there an hour earlier.

"It just feels a little strange," she murmured, but he noticed how her lips softened as she looked down at her hand, moving her fingers slightly so the stone caught the afternoon sunlight. "But it's beautiful."

"Suits you," he replied automatically, taking her arm to cross the street. "Almost as much as that forget-me-not underwear."

The compliment and/or teasing brought color to Emily's cheeks, but she didn't comment. She'd been quiet all afternoon—no, longer. Ever since they left Plenty for the city earlier that morning.

"So, you're glad I persuaded you to get a ring?" he persisted, keeping hold of her arm when she tried to reclaim it at the other side of the street. He leaned down closer to her ear. "Or did you at least enjoy my means of persuasion?"

Predictably her blush deepened and—even more predictably—Mitch's body reacted. For the past ten days since she'd said 'yes', he'd applied many and various means of persuasion, and now here they were in Sydney, with a ring on her finger, a registry office earmarked and a date penciled in. All they needed was one last piece of paperwork, and by the end of the day that, too, would be settled. He hunched his shoulders against a sudden chill in his flesh. Five hours and it would all be over. Finished. Done.

A group of tourists spilled out of a hotel into their path, and Mitch tucked Emily closer to his side as he guided her around their perimeter. Her body bumped against his with every step, warm and giving and...tense? He glanced down, saw her flicking at the ring with her thumbnail.

"If it's not the ring," he began, frowning at the nervous gesture, "is it the registry office? Didn't you like it?"

"No, it was fine. Nicer than I thought, with the pews and flowers and everything. It's...it's stupid." She made a small, dismissive sound. "Prewedding jitters, I suppose."

If she meant those dark-of-night, gut-twisting attacks of self-doubt—*Why am I doing this? How can I make her happy? What will I do if she leaves me, too?*—then he understood. "It'll be okay once we get these formalities over with."

"I guess." But she didn't sound very convinced, and Mitch wondered if the speed things were moving had spooked her. Dinner tonight, somewhere classy, he decided as he ushered her down the side street toward where he'd parked the SUV. Her SUV, that she'd only driven around the countryside. Perhaps she needed a distraction from whatever troubled her. At least with two hands on the wheel she'd be forced to stop worrying her ring to death.

"How about you drive?" he asked, fishing for the keys. "There won't be too much traffic this time of day."

"I'd rather not."

"I'd rather you did." He released her arm, but only so he could press the keys into her hand. He closed her stiff fingers around them. "You said you wanted to try."

With her head bowed, he couldn't see her face, but he could feel the tension in her fingers. "Yes, I do, absolutely, but this isn't the best time."

"Good a time as any." He released her hand and stepped back. "Come on, Emily, stop thinking about it and just do it. Open the door and get in the seat. Once you start, you'll be fine."

"It's not the driving, Mitch." She blew out a breath that sounded a little shaky around the edges, and the keys jingled a nervous, metallic dance as she shifted them from one hand to the other. "It's not going very well, this getting married business, is it?"

"Hey." He cupped her face in his palm, brushed his thumb across her cheekbone. "This getting married business is almost done."

When she opened her mouth to respond, her lips trembled, and Mitch's breath backed up in his lungs. Damn, he hated these tremory spells. Hated his feeling of helplessness even as he shushed her second attempt to speak and drew her against his chest, not tightly, but in a loose-armed grip that gave her space to move. Space to retreat if she didn't want his embrace. Lately the only place he knew what she wanted was in his bed, and that thought didn't thrill him half as much as it ought. He wanted…hell, all he wanted was for this strange new state of their relationship to settle, to establish a pattern where he knew what to expect.

A gust of wind swirled down the street, stirring Emily's loose hair so it whipped across his throat and teased his jaw and chin. That fleeting touch combined with the scent of her shampoo to set up a warm ache in his chest, right where her head lay against his leather jacket. Then her hands shifted, sliding under his jacket to rest on his waist, one flat and warming all the way through his shirt, one fisted to hold the car keys.

It was the simplest touch, not teasing or suggestive, but natural and…trusting. The ache in his chest tightened, then it shifted and swelled like a wave, knocking his feet out from under him. Not what he wanted, this terrifying wash of response to what should have been an uncomplicated embrace. Not what he'd envisaged, when he'd asked her to be his wife.

Tension stiffened his posture in a reflexive reaction, and her head lifted a little. Enough that he could rest his hands on her shoulders and exert sufficient pressure to peel her all the way clear of his body. Good. Great. Now he could breathe again. He wasn't missing that soft, warm pressure at all.

"Better now?" he asked.

"Yes and no." Her hands fidgeted with the same ambivalence as her answer, juggling the keys, ducking into her jacket pockets and out again, almost as

if she didn't know what to do with them now that
they weren't on him.

"The answer's obviously no." And he took those
restless hands in his, steadying them. "You think we
should talk about whatever it is that's bothering
you?"

"I'm afraid if I start talking I'll never stop, and
that is *so* not what you want."

Dread settled heavy in Mitch's gut, but he had to
ask, "Why is that?"

"You seem to think I'm this practical and even-
tempered person, and I have no idea why." She blew
out an exasperated breath. "I just feel like this giant
emotion-filled balloon, and every day something ex-
pands it a bit more. Every other minute I think I'm
going to explode."

"How about you let it go one puff at a time."
Mitch squeezed her hands. "Come on, Emily, one
thing."

For a second she resisted, shaking her head and
trying to pull her hands free. But then she sucked in
an audible breath and said, "So, okay, I'm not so
happy about the registry office."

"You said it was fine."

"And so it is. I'm sure it's finer than most registry
offices, but—"

"You don't want to get married there." Mitch let
go of her hands so he could put his own on his hips.
He shook his head. "Why didn't you just say so?"

"Because I was trying to make it easier on you,"
she fired back. "I know your first wedding was a big,
church affair and I didn't want to remind you of it."

"It's not something I'm likely to forget."

"I know that." She shook her head, almost sadly,

regretfully. "And I wish that didn't bother me as much as it does, but I know you'll never let go of Annabelle's memory."

"I can't change my history," he said stiffly, although God knows he wished he could. "I have a failed marriage and I won't ever forget that."

"And you think that's your fault, don't you? You blame yourself for her leaving, for deserting Joshua, when the decision was hers." Eyes narrowed and brimful of passion, she leaned closer, and her voice dropped to a new, low intensity. "Nothing you could have done would have changed her mind, Mitch. You can't hold yourself responsible for the choices she made."

"Maybe I don't," he said softly, although he knew her parents held him responsible and that's why they'd kept their distance. Why they chose to contact him through a law office. He reached out and plucked the car keys from her hand. "But that's not something I'm going to debate with you on a city street."

"Is it something you'll ever debate?" she asked, not giving an inch.

"What are you asking, Emily?" Hands on hips he glared down at her. "If you expect me to forget about my first marriage, you're asking too much."

She eyed him narrowly a moment longer, and something shifted in her eyes, like a new understanding or a decision made, before she nodded slowly. "I can see that."

"Good," he said while all kinds of not-good alarms sounded in his head. "Now you've got that out, I'll take you home."

Home would have been lovely, Emily thought an hour later. Anywhere would have been preferable to the chic, beachside apartment he had shared with Annabelle, but that's where he took her and that's where he left her while he went to meet with the Blainey's lawyer. From the bathroom window she watched him climb into a taxi—easier, he'd said, than parking in the city—and her spirits bottomed right out.

She had thought it couldn't get much worse than that silent ride through the suburbs, until she walked into this place with Annabelle's touches in every room, on every wall, in the very air she breathed. Had she really thought he would forget his first wife so easily? Had she actually believed that the magic she'd felt in his arms and his bed was mutual?

Apparently she had, unless the acute ache in her chest was due to something other than the splintered pieces of her heart. She couldn't marry him, not even for the security of his home or to belong in his fabulous family—without his love, that would be meaningless. And as for a baby...

Emily swung away from the window. There was no baby, she'd discovered this morning, so why torture herself with that particular question? She should be glad, pleased that she'd arrived at this painful decision while she still had choices—while she could still walk away.

Walk away? She shook her head ruefully as she wandered into the kitchen. Where could she walk to? Practically speaking, she was holed up here in this hated apartment, a prisoner of her own weaknesses. Why hadn't she told him she wouldn't stay here? Why hadn't she stamped her foot and demanded to go home, back to Korringal? That's what his beloved Annabelle would have done.

But no, Emily Warner did not do tantrums. She conceded and she allowed herself to be persuaded and she held her simmering emotions in check because she wanted love so desperately. So here she stood, alone and fraught and on the brink of screaming.

Not crying. She was too afraid that if she started, she would never stop.

She was alone and fraught, PMSy and empty. And although she knew that last had nothing to do with her stomach, she opened the pantry doors and studied the paltry contents. Nothing resembling chocolate. Nothing that looked remotely capable of satisfying the hollow ache in her soul.

And then, lurking in the farthest corner, she found the one and only promising item—a can of full-fat, sweetened condensed milk—and set to it with a can opener. The fancy European contraption refused to cooperate. It slid off the rim, it skimmed across the top, and finally it clattered to the floor.

Talk about the last straw. Emily lifted the can in her hand and the urge to hurl it screamed through her body. Except she didn't have a beef with either the can or the wall that would bear its brunt. Her frustrated anger wasn't even with Annabelle for casting aside everything Emily most desired, or with Mitch for his blind stubbornness.

No, she was mad as hell for allowing herself to be a victim, for inviting circumstances to come up and take a big bite. She was mad enough to grab her overnight bag and her car keys and head for the door…but not so mad that she didn't pause to jot a note.

Then she strode out the door into the cold winter night. She didn't know where she was going, but she could not stay here a minute longer.

* * *

Mitch exited the lawyer's office and let his breath go on a long sigh. Relief, closure, satisfaction—a whole myriad of emotions rolled through him as he paused to study the envelope in his hand. His ex-wife's death certificate, the last piece of documentation necessary for him to marry Emily, and getting it had been surprisingly easy...surprising because he'd expected some glitch. Nothing about his dealings with Annabelle had ever been simple.

A corner of his mouth twisted as he recalled that scene with Emily earlier in the day. Nothing with her was turning out easy, either, and he needed to start figuring out a way to simplify things instead of complicating them every time he opened his mouth. Uneasiness stirred through him, a vague sense of...hell, he didn't know what, but it sent him striding out into the foyer. His head came up, startled, when he saw the burly figure pacing the corridor outside.

"Randall."

The man halted, expelled a harsh breath. "You got what you came for?"

"Yes." And Mitch could have kept going—almost did keep going—but for the pain etched on his ex-father-in-law's face. Not an easy thing for him, knowing what the envelope in Mitch's hand contained. "I'm sorry I had to ask for this."

Something flickered across Randall's face, eased in his stiff posture. He nodded. "I wasn't going to come here—Janet didn't even want me to hand over the certificate. She was the one who couldn't meet with you that day you came to the lodge."

"She still blames me?"

"She still...hurts."

Mitch remembered Janet Blainey's hurt very clearly, even on some level understood that she'd needed to lash out, to direct it at someone. "And you?"

"The rawness has healed enough to see things more clearly," Randall said candidly. "You weren't responsible for her choices. I hope you know that."

"A couple of hours ago someone else told me the same thing."

"Did you listen?"

"I should have."

Yeah, he should have listened, and to more than the words rolling from Emily's tongue. He should have listened to the things left unspoken, to the silent message in his heart. He should have started listening a long time ago.

"I know Joshua would love to see you and his grandmother. I left my contact details with your lawyer, but I'd prefer to deal directly with you and Janet." He offered his hand. "I'm glad you did come here today."

"Me, too, Mitch. Me, too." The other man's eyes glinted with moisture as he accepted the handshake, a gesture that felt like closure on past understandings and a new beginning.

That notion settled inside Mitch, a remarkably comfortable fit that hurried his progress out into the street. Suddenly he needed to be home, with Emily, listening to his heart. As he hailed a taxi, the cool splash of rain on his face turned his gaze to the evening sky. He hadn't even noticed that it was starting to rain.

Mitch saw the vacant car space where he'd parked the SUV beside his truck earlier in the day, and alarm sliced through him, chillingly sharp. Surely she hadn't taken it into her head to go driving, not with night falling with the same sudden, winter speed as the rain. Unable to wait for the elevator, he took the stairs to the third floor two at a time while his heart bumped against his ribs with the frantic beat of fear.

He flicked the light switch as he came through the door, and the sudden burst of illumination caught the note on the hall stand, anchored by a can of milk. Mitch went cold, ice-cold. For one numb moment he couldn't move, couldn't feel, couldn't see anything beyond that single sheet of white paper, the same as she'd left before.

No, not the same as last time. He let the door fall shut behind him with a solid thunk that mobilized his stalled mind and heart and limbs. This time he wasn't letting her go. This time he would find her, this time—

His gut clenched with renewed fear as he scanned the short note. She had taken the SUV. Heart racing, he strode to the phone and tapped out her cell phone number with a clumsy, leaden finger. Twice he had to stop and start again. Then he chanted, "Come on, come on," as he waited through ring after ring after ring. An interminable time that stretched his nerves to snapping point before the ringing stopped and he heard her soft voice.

"Hello."

"Thank God." He pressed a hand to his forehead, to the light-headed spinning relief. "Where are you?"

"Didn't you get my note?"

"Yeah, I got your note. What the hell possessed—" He sucked in a breath and forced himself to resume in a more reasonable tone. "Just tell me where you are, and I'll come and get you."

The beat of a pause stretched between them before she said, "There's no need—I'm fine. No, I'm better than fine. I've just driven from one side of Sydney to the other." In her voice he heard dawning wonder and a growing strength of purpose. "I did it by myself and I'm going to keep on doing that."

"Emily, be sensible and—"

"You know, Mitch," she interrupted, "I'm not that sensible, and I'm not always practical and I'm very rarely even tempered. Basically, I'm not the person you want to marry."

Stunned, Mitch sat. Held his spinning head a second before his temper flared again. "You're wrong, damn it. You are the only person I want to marry."

But he was listening to a dial tone. She'd not only run away, she'd hung up on him. A tight, edgy smile curled Mitch's lips as he strode back to the hall stand and grabbed the keys to his truck. For once he didn't mind the sharp irritation that blazed through his blood. It kept the icy bite of terror at bay.

Driving back to Plenty through the misty rain, Mitch's temper didn't stand a chance against the insidious chill of dread. By the time he pulled into the Korringal yard, his bones ached with fear. The house sat in darkness, no lights, so when he saw the SUV parked in its half of the double garage, overwhelming relief quashed any remnant anger.

She was home.

But not in her room, he discovered with a pang of alarm. A half-unpacked bag sat on her bed with several of her many bears, but not Emily. He found her two minutes later, curled up asleep in his bed, and his whole being surged with intense emotion even as he slumped against the doorjamb.

His first impulse was to haul back the bedclothes, climb in beside her, and wrap her tightly in his arms. His second exercised more restraint. For several seconds he stood beside the bed and simply watched her. Here, safe in his bed. He didn't know what that meant, but it had to be good.

Then he flicked on the bedside lamp and sat on the side of the bed, touching the fine silk of her hair where it spread across his pillow, her cheek, her brow, and—as she slowly came awake—her sleepy smile of recognition. That welcome turned his heart.

"You're home," she said, her voice as soft as that smile.

"So are you, and I can't tell you how thankful I am." Remnant fear still shivered through his blood, reminding him, roughening his voice when he continued. "Don't ever run away again, Em. I don't ever want to walk in the door to one of those notes again."

Something shifted in her eyes, a different kind of recognition, as she came fully awake. When she started to wriggle, trying to sit up, he pinned her under the tightly stretched bedclothes with a hand each side of her shoulders.

He held her gaze steadily and Emily swallowed. It didn't seem possible that she could have woken to find Mitch here, leaning over her, eyes glowing with something that looked like... No, she had to be dreaming. *Somebody pinch me.*

"You're not running away or hanging up," he said firmly. "You're staying right there while we talk a few things through. Right to the end of the conversation this time.''

So, okay, a metaphorical pinch would do the trick. She definitely was not dreaming, yet the reality did not faze her. She had driven all the way from Sydney in the rain, and she felt strong and proud, as if nothing could daunt her ever again.

''What happened?'' Mitch asked quietly. ''Why did you decide to take your first city drive on a wet night?''

''After our disagreement, I got good and mad and I couldn't stay in that apartment. I couldn't just sit and not do something positive, something for myself. I decided to take that drive, although I didn't know where I was going until you called.''

''You sound pretty pleased with yourself.''

''I am.'' A smile hovered around the corners of her mouth, just bursting to get out. ''I did it, Mitch. I conquered those demons all by myself, and it feels very good.''

''Not sensible, not practical, but…good.''

Was he teasing? Hard to tell with his face darkly shadowed. Regardless, Emily wanted to explain—she needed him to understand. ''About that…what I said on the phone. I know I've always strived to be the kind of person you described. I guess I went overboard trying to please my mother, my family, whoever. But that's not who I am, not in my heart, and I'm sick of acting calm and even and practical when I'm churning up inside.''

He touched her cheek. ''If you hadn't hung up, you would know what I think of who you are.''

Definitely not teasing now. There was no laughter

in his eyes, just solemn purpose. "I didn't want to argue with you," she said.

"Then don't. Just listen to what you missed." As if to illustrate his seriousness, he pressed his fingers against her lips. "I do want to marry you, Emily, but not for the reasons I thought. When I held you this morning, when you put your head against my chest and your hands on my waist, what I was feeling—"

He broke off, shaking his head and the rough edge to his voice, the depth of emotion in his eyes, sent Emily's hopeful heart soaring.

"I should have told you then. I shouldn't have let things between us slide, but I was overwhelmed. Terrified. And I just wanted to get that lawyer's appointment over with."

"Did you see Annabelle's parents?" she managed.

"Randall, afterward, and that was good. Things will be all right," he said, almost offhand, as if she'd diverted him from his purpose. Then he focused again, his gaze strong and intent on her face. "But that's not what the appointment was about. I needed her death certificate, Em, so we can marry."

Oh, dear Lord. No wonder he'd been tense, edgy. Emily's heart ached for him, and she struggled to free her arms, her hands, wanting to touch him, hold him, but he leaned closer, keeping her trapped.

"It wasn't the greatest time for me to experience these huge feelings, to know I was about to put my heart out there and risk another failure." His eyes, steady on hers, were filled with hope, full of promises. "I love you, Emily, even though I didn't want to feel like this about anyone."

"Again," she added softly.

"No, not again. How I feel about you is unique."

Then, as if he saw the objection, the question, the lingering doubt in her eyes, he bent down and kissed her, a brief, tender melding of lips that sang in Emily's blood.

"I stopped loving Annabelle a long time ago—I don't think I ever loved her enough—but I kept trying for Joshua's sake and because of my own stubborn pride. It took me a long time to accept that the marriage was finished, and just when I did...the accident."

And that terrible, dark night when Emily had yearned to ease his anguish.

"Why did you run away?" he asked, and she didn't know if he had read her thoughts, or which particular "running away" he meant. It didn't matter—the same answer applied.

"Because I loved you, Mitch. I couldn't stay." And it was her turn to quiet his protest with a telling look. Her turn to spill her heart. "I loved that ridiculous sense of honor that wouldn't let you take advantage of me even when you were drunk. I even loved you for trying to save your marriage, but I didn't think you would ever love me. Not in the way I yearned for.... I can't believe that you do."

Toward the end her voice started to waver, and when he told her to, "Believe it, sweetheart, it's true," her eyes, like her heart, overflowed with joy.

"For pity's sake," she said, with a very unromantic sniff, "I can't seem to stop these tears lately. If I ever do get pregnant, I can't imagine the hormonal waterworks."

The hand he lifted to brush away those tears paused. "You're not...?" and when she shook her head, he added an emphatic, "Good."

Emily's heart stalled. He really sounded as if he meant it. "You don't want a baby?"

"What I don't want is you marrying me to have a baby, or because you're having one. I want you to have choices, Em, always, and I realize I've messed up, big-time, in that department."

"You're doing a pretty passable job of making up for it," she said, meeting his eyes, smiling through the tears.

"I hope like hell you choose to marry me, to be my wife, but it needs to be your choice. Because you love me and want to spend the rest of your life with me. If you want to get married on the top of Mount Tibaroo wearing ski suits, then we'll do it. However, wherever. Your choice."

Emily huffed out a breath, speechless, completely blown away. "Would it be all right," she managed, eventually, "if I choose to be let free of this straitjacket? Because I really need to be held right now."

And when he did let her free of the restraining blankets, when his arms were wrapped around her and her head lay cradled against his shoulder, she told him that there was no choice to make. She told him she loved him but hated ski suits and she told him, again, how much she loved him, and then she laughed with pure happiness, laughed even though the tears were spilling from her eyes and he was holding her so tight she would probably be bruised. Then she considered asking him to pinch her, but didn't.

This was no dream. This was real, this man, this love, this future. Real and strong and hers.

Epilogue

Emily chose a spring wedding in Julia's garden. When Chantal and Julia couldn't agree on bridesmaids' dresses, she calmly and practically ditched the idea of attendants…except for Joshua, who carried the rings and didn't argue at all. Chantal did get to organize everything from the eighty handwritten invitations to the reception food to the teddy bear wedding favors. She did not choose the music.

Mitch added another arrow to his writer's quiver, penning a personalized service with twin themes: success and choice. As a wedding present, he handed his bride the deed to her grandfather's house. Emily gifted her husband with news of her pregnancy, and when *A Risky Business* hit number one on three bestseller lists, she organized a surprise celebration complete with one of Julia's special cakes.

After the last guests left, Mitch planned on playing

out his raspberries-and-cream fantasy. Instead he rushed his wife to the maternity ward of Cliffton Private Hospital. Much to Joshua's delight, the baby was a boy.

*   *   *   *   *

If you enjoyed what you just read,
then we've got an offer you can't resist!

Take 2 bestselling
love stories FREE!
Plus get a FREE surprise gift!

Clip this page and mail it to Silhouette Reader Service™

IN U.S.A.
3010 Walden Ave.
P.O. Box 1867
Buffalo, N.Y. 14240-1867

IN CANADA
P.O. Box 609
Fort Erie, Ontario
L2A 5X3

YES! Please send me 2 free Silhouette Desire® novels and my free surprise gift. After receiving them, if I don't wish to receive anymore, I can return the shipping statement marked cancel. If I don't cancel, I will receive 6 brand-new novels every month, before they're available in stores! In the U.S.A., bill me at the bargain price of $3.57 plus 25¢ shipping and handling per book and applicable sales tax, if any*. In Canada, bill me at the bargain price of $4.24 plus 25¢ shipping and handling per book and applicable taxes**. That's the complete price and a savings of at least 10% off the cover prices—what a great deal! I understand that accepting the 2 free books and gift places me under no obligation ever to buy any books. I can always return a shipment and cancel at any time. Even if I never buy another book from Silhouette, the 2 free books and gift are mine to keep forever.

225 SDN DNUP
326 SDN DNUQ

Name	(PLEASE PRINT)	
Address	Apt.#	
City	State/Prov.	Zip/Postal Code

* Terms and prices subject to change without notice. Sales tax applicable in N.Y.
** Canadian residents will be charged applicable provincial taxes and GST.
   All orders subject to approval. Offer limited to one per household and not valid to
   current Silhouette Desire® subscribers.
   ® are registered trademarks of Harlequin Books S.A., used under license.

DES02   ©1998 Harlequin Enterprises Limited

The captivating family saga of the Danforths continues with

SCANDAL BETWEEN THE SHEETS
by
Brenda Jackson
(Silhouette Desire #1573)

There was one thing more seductive to hotshot reporter
Jasmine Carmody than a career-making story: tall, dark
businessman Wesley Brooks. But Wesley had his own
agenda, and would do whatever it took to ensure Jasmine
didn't uncover the scandal surrounding his close friends, the
Danforths…even if it meant getting closer still to Jasmine!

DYNASTIES: THE DANFORTHS

**A family of prominence…
tested by scandal, sustained by passion!**

Available April 2004 at your favorite retail outlet.

COMING NEXT MONTH

#1573 SCANDAL BETWEEN THE SHEETS—Brenda Jackson
Dynasties: The Danforths
There was one thing more seductive to hotshot reporter Jasmine Carmody than a career-making story: tall, dark businessman Wesley Brooks. But Wesley had his own agenda, and would do whatever it took to ensure Jasmine didn't uncover the scandal surrounding his close friends, the Danforths…even if it meant getting *closer* still to Jasmine!

#1574 KEEPING BABY SECRET—Beverly Barton
The Protectors
The sexual chemistry had been explosive between Lurleen "Leenie" Patton and Frank Latimer. And their brief but passionate affair had resulted in a baby…a son Frank knew nothing about. When tragedy struck and their child was kidnapped, Leenie needed Frank to help find their son. But first she had to tell Frank he was a father….

#1575 A KEPT WOMAN—Sheri WhiteFeather
Mixing business and pleasure was against the rules for U.S. Marshal Zack Ryder. But Natalie Pascal—the very witness he was supposed to be protecting—tempted him beyond reason. The vulnerable vixen hid from a painful past, and Zack told himself he was only offering her comfort with his kisses, his touch….

#1576 FIT FOR A SHEIKH—Kristi Gold
Texas Cattleman's Club: The Stolen Baby
Sheikh Darin Shakir was on a mission to find and bring to justice a dangerous fugitive who used Las Vegas as his playground. But unforeseen circumstances had left Darin with bartending beauty Fiona Powers as his Sin City tour guide. Together, they were hot on the trail of the bad guy…and getting even hotter for each other!

#1577 SLOW DANCING WITH A TEXAN—Linda Conrad
Making time for men was never a concern for workaholic Lainie Gardner. That is, until a scary brush with a stalker forced her into hiding. Now, deep in the wilderness with her temporary bodyguard, Texas Ranger Sloan Abbot, the sexual tension sizzled. Could Lainie give in to her deepest desires for the headstrong cowboy?

#1578 A PASSIONATE PROPOSAL—Emilie Rose
Teacher Tracy Sullivan had had a crash on surgical resident Cort Lander *forever*. But when the sexy single dad hired *her* on as his baby's nanny, things got a little more heated. Tracy decided that getting over her crush meant giving in to passion…but would a no-strings-attached affair pave the way for a love beyond her wildest dreams?

SDCNM0304